"NOW, OCHOA, GRAB CAIN'S OTHER HAND."
Once she did and the Third had spread to connect the
three of us together, I pushed us through the wall. As
I emerged into another dark expanse, my confidence
waned, and I was afraid I would turn around to see Cain
or Ochoa stuck in the wall. But they both squeezed my
hands in reassurance, and a huge sigh of relief escaped
my lips.

"Would have been helpful to have known before that
it worked that way," Cain muttered.

"It wouldn't have. What happened has changed me,"
I said.

But that conversation was put on hold as Cain and
Ochoa turned up the lights on their suits and illuminated the darkness.

We'd stepped directly into hell.

THE THREE-FOLD SUNS

THE SECRETS OF EPO-5

OF

EPO-5

THE THREE-FOLD SUNS

Book 4

by

ELIZABETH
KNOLLSTON

ISBN Paperback: 978-1-959159-08-7
ISBN Ebook: 978-1-959159-09-4

Cover Art and Interior Design © Elizabeth Knollston
Editing by Red Adept Editing Services

Published by Lewis Bros. Press
PO Box 261
Larned, KS 67550

www.elizabethknollston.com

for Katie
who has been a fantasic
sounding board for ideas
and a wonderful
cheerleader as I get close
to the finish line

1

Confinement

Being confined to a shuttle—designed for two individuals but stuffed with five—for a little over two weeks wasn't conducive to prepping for meeting up with a traitor and a nemesis. Nor was there much privacy or food, which was the critical factor. Cain had given me a wicked grin as he negotiated for zip pockets to be our sole source of nutrients. Thank Jupiter for Miles, who'd insisted on having his chef whip up a fresh batch of zips—full of delicious ingredients and not the foul-smelling items Cain had eaten on Epsilon's Station.

All of the *Samaritan*'s shuttles were equipped with food dispensers, but in order to reach Epo-5 as quickly as possible, the engineers had reconfigured any system we could safely do without, in order to provide more power to the miniature overdrive engine. Captain Lio had insisted on letting the best technicians and engineers on board the *Samaritan* spend three days maxing out the shuttle's engine capabilities.

"What's our ETA?" I asked.

Cain sighed. "For the hundredth time, we'll be at

Rockerton's in"—he half stood and glanced over Lieutenant Chambers's shoulder—"three hours and twenty-nine minutes."

My lack of space to pace had set me on edge within the first hours of leaving the *Samaritan*. Thank the universe Cain and I had turned a corner in our relationship, because the man was showing an unceasing amount of patience with me. I wasn't sure our other three bunkmates felt the same way.

Lio had stayed true to his word and assigned three of his crew members to go with us to Epo-5. I understood his rationale, but I would have preferred just Cain and I go. Lieutenant Chambers and Lieutenant Aj-Otha were former military, and Lieutenant Commander Ochoa was former IGJ intelligence.

I'd peeked at their files before we left. If we were going to become insta-best buds, I wanted to know who I was dealing with.

I trusted Lio, but the InterGalactic Justice system had left a nasty taste in my mouth after they tortured Cain, and I dealt with Commandant Yilmaz. When I read through Ochoa's background, I'd confessed my breach of protocol to Lio. He was annoyed but ended up sharing a personal and touching moment between the two of them, which boiled down to the fact he trusted Ochoa with his life. So I continued to place my trust in Lio.

"Remember, the two you of are to stay on the shuttle," Ochoa said.

I rolled my eyes.

"I saw that," she muttered.

<Are you sure she's not part Darquet?> I asked Cain.

He grinned and shook his head.

"We'll be in and out before you know it," Aj-Otha said. He twisted in his seat to give me a smile. If not for the four rows of sharp teeth he sported, his smile might have been reassuring.

I'd had little to no dealings with a Quiloto before. They were fiercely loyal and equipped with a pair of wings. Aj-Otha had had his bioenhanced. Each wing had been surgically overlaid with a thin sheet of enhanced magnesium alloy. A plethora of sensors laced his wings, all tied into his neural implants.

"We'll get the data packets," Ochoa assured me.

I leaned back into the corner of the shuttle I'd claimed as mine and tried to relax. We'd decided direct communication among us, the *Samaritan*, and Miles was too risky. We all needed to fly dark, which meant those of us in the shuttle would have only one opportunity for an update before we reached Epo-5, at Rockerton's All-in-One Fueling Station, a free-floating asteroid the Rockerton family had converted a few generations back. It was the only place the shuttle would pass without having to detour and rack up major time delays. Lio and Miles had both promised updates for us by the time we reached Rockerton's.

I was nervous about stopping there, even though we needed intel. But we had to get to Epo-5 before Yilmaz and Dr. Sia-Al Ashter did. As each day wore on, I lost my optimism about beating them to the planet.

Cain did his best to reassure me. <*We don't know that they've made it there yet. Lio or Miles will have an update waiting for us. Then we can make the appropriate plans.*>

<And if Yilmaz and Dr. Ashter have figured it out already? What then?> My stomach rolled, and my chest tightened. I could feel Cain's longing to hold me, to comfort me. But we were keeping anything physical to a bare minimum, not even holding hands, although the others were likely well aware of our newfound connection, thanks to Miles and his little gossip train.

I let my head fall back against the shuttle's wall and sorted through the tangled mess of information. *Would have been far easier if you'd just been up front with me, Pops.* I couldn't believe only a couple of months had passed since I boarded the *Rapscallion*. That felt like a lifetime ago. But enough time had passed that I could slip back into the memories of the nightmare-filled tour without too much anxiety: Mrs. Gol and her dead son, Triton; the Star Eaters; the beginning of my relationship with Cain; and the shock of realizing I hadn't known my pops at all.

Why did you hide this from me? I couldn't help but wonder if Pops had shared more with Lucas or if Lucas had picked up on things I'd missed. My brain screamed those scenarios were the likely answer, given Lucas's recent actions—the timing of his popping back into my life was more than coincidence. And even though I wanted nothing to do with his crazed killing spree, the thought of being excluded still stung.

Was I not worthy? That was a loaded question and probably unfair to ask of myself. The Star Eaters had gotten Miles to inject me with modified smart-bots, which the Third had replaced on our eventful excursion to Dar. If that was indeed what Mrs. Gol and her ilk had been working toward for generations, then I was more than worthy. *Did you know that, Pops? Or was that why you never included me?* Maybe he'd figured it all out by then and hadn't wanted me to be a part of the experiments. *Maybe you acted the way you did in order to save me.*

That idea didn't sit well because if that was the case, then he'd killed all those people for me—not some mystical reason for teaming up with the Eeri, just the simple reason of a father wanting to protect his daughter.

A shiver ran up and down my spine.

Cain stood, shuffled over to me, then squeezed himself between Ochoa's chair and me. His hand found mine, and he laced his fingers through my own.

I gave him a questioning look. *<I thought we'd agreed on no touchy-feely.>*

<That was before. This is now. Whatever your father did, he alone is responsible for—not you.>

I squeezed my eyes shut and let my head slide down to rest on his shoulder. *<Easier said than done.>* I didn't want to step on that emotional land mine. But I couldn't help it. We were almost at Epo-5, the planet all roads seemed to point to. The mysterious way the Third tried to communicate had reminded me of what I'd seen as a kid when Pops was working on Epo-5, not to mention his cryptic—well, maybe not as cryptic as he'd hoped—letter that had hinted at the miserable waste heap of a world.

The answers to my pops's actions had been floating along in my periphery for the past couple of months. And my gut was telling me they were ready to take center stage. I just needed to be ready to face them, whatever they turned out to be, because I had to believe the answer to what Lucas was up to was somewhere in there, along with this mysterious connection among the Star Eaters, the Third, and me.

Since the destruction of Starbase 9.2, Cloud 11, and Lunar 5, my brother had been relatively quiet. The rest of the known worlds hadn't been. The Jumjul had taken action. They'd initiated a martial control clause, which they'd sneaked into several of their written alliances with various worlds, and they'd clarified that humanity was going to be held responsible if Lucas and his followers weren't stopped within the next few weeks. That deadline was forcing the Old Earth Monarchy to respond and not too well either. The emperor hadn't even tried to mask his contempt for the Jumjul and their threats and had clearly stated Lucas wasn't Old Earth's problem. He turned the blame toward the IGJ.

We'd left the *Samaritan* before Commandant Yilmaz broadcast a reply. The only nice thought I could muster about the woman was that she would have more diplomatic grace than the emperor, at least. And maybe, just maybe, this whole Jumjul threat would demand too much of her attention and slow her down on her way to Epo-5. *Fingers crossed. And toes.*

I closed my eyes and tried to conjure up a few happy memories to take my mind off everything. Studying the files we'd brought was no-go for me at present. I'd pored over them until my vision swam, and my mind was throwing out wildly unhelpful ideas. Cain told me to stop, and after a bit of an argument, I'd decided he might have a point.

But even the happy memories were tough because all roads led back to Pops—even memories of Cain—because without Pops's actions, I would never have worked for Confore Tech, earning the voucher for the cruise on the *Starshine*, being mistaken for helping Jorge uncover Confore and Yilmaz's partnership over Project Clear Sight and the SeeClear tech, and having Cain come into my life. Everything was a complicated mess of questions, doubts, and fears.

I gripped Cain's hand a little more tightly and tried hard to focus on something else, anything else.

In my mind, a field of luscious green grass filled with wildflowers of every color sprang to life. Off in the distance was a stand of trees, and beyond that, the purplish hint of mountains. A soft summer breeze swept across the meadow, and I could hear the grasses gently brushing up against one another. Underneath were the faint hums and chirps of insects, and far above me, a bird cried out. Sunshine filled the meadow, and its warmth moved across my skin.

For a moment, I resisted getting lost in the scene's beauty. *Am I having visions again?* I'd been running on the assumption the Third had left me. When we'd been underground, trying to rescue Elea, Cain's sister, and the Holy One had shown up, the Third that had attached itself to me had gone after the Darquet. *But I had another vision after that, didn't I? When the tunnel had collapsed. But if this is the Third trying to communicate with me, why now? And why choose something so—*

<*Just let yourself relax.*> Cain's thoughts interrupted my own. <*This is a memory of a favorite place when I was young.*

My father would sometimes take Elea and me to Culi when he needed a break from my mother.>

<You can project memories now?>

<It would appear that way.> A smug pride tucked between his words, but I snuggled closer and worked through a few deep-breathing exercises.

<Tell me a story. Something from your childhood,> I sent.

Cain's hand brushed back a few strands of hair that had fallen over my face, and he let his head rest on mine. *<My father loved insects. He trained to be an entomologist, with additional specialties in ecosystems and bioseeding. I think he learned to love and cherish the delicate balance of an ecosystem from his father, who passed down stories of when his father had lived on Dar. So when he needed a break from the political life, he always escaped back to nature. And Culi was his favorite.>*

Cain continued to share until I drifted off to sleep. And I dreamed of a young boy running through the meadow, laughing and chasing winged insects through an endless sea of color.

2

Embarrassing Nightmares

Somewhere in my dreams, the young boy, all smiles and giggles, morphed into my brother. Lucas was young, his skin smudged with foul sludge, and the whites of his eyes visible and fearful. He was running and tripping through muck as though chased by a nightmare of his own.

I jerked awake, screaming.

The walls of the shuttle were melting, a sickly green slime burning through the metal. Slumped over in their chairs, Ochoa and Aj-Otha's flesh bubbled and boiled while Chambers, seated on the floor across from me, was tearing at his face, screaming as he ripped away pieces of skin. I turned toward Cain—still seated next to me—but instead of his reassuring gaze, all that stared back was an eyeless husk of the man he'd once been.

I tried to scoot back, to get as far away from his corpse as I could, but the shuttle was too small. My hands touched the slime on the walls, and I could feel it eat through—

"Wake up!" Cain's voice boomed.

Someone had grabbed me and was shaking me, but I couldn't open my eyes, no matter how I struggled. Then I felt a sharp prick at the base of my neck, and everything melted away into a sea of darkness.

"Vitals?" Cain was asking someone.

"Faint but steady. The neurodepressant did the job. Now we let her wake up on—"

My eyes fluttered open, and I cringed. I didn't know if I was going to wake to a nightmare turned into reality or reality restored. My eyes focused on the worried but thankfully fully fleshed face of Chambers. And next to him was Cain, his eyes amber with flecks of black.

"Mahia? Can you hear me?" Chambers asked softly.

I nodded. "Loud and clear, Doc."

Chambers boasted not only formal military experience on his record but a medical degree as well. *Who would've guessed I would have a mini meltdown? Evidently, Lio.* That was one reason he made an excellent captain.

"Can you tell me what happened?"

I tried to push myself up and felt a pair of hands assist me. "Don't move too much," Cain said.

"I'm all right. Promise," I said, trying to wave him off.

<Liar.>

Maybe. As the foul taste of the nightmare cleared, all I really felt was embarrassment.

I blushed at Chambers's intent gaze and looked away. I opened and closed my hands a few times and noted they felt tight, as if they'd fallen asleep and I'd gone straight past the tingly stage into the puffy stage. "It was nothing. Really. Just a bad dream."

Chambers frowned and glanced at Cain. "With every-thing you've been through, I'm not surprised. Frankly, I would have expected you to have been having night-mares for weeks by now."

"Everything okay?" Ochoa asked. "We need to broadcast for clearance to land. If we're still going to do that."

Ochoa held seniority, but she'd been deferring to Cain and me on most decisions. I appreciated that.

"Yes. We need the updates," I said. "Could I have some water?"

Chambers nodded and rotated to dig through the supply packs. He pulled out an edible water bottle. "Here. Drink it then eat it. The electrolytes and boosted vit-mins will be good for your body right now."

I shook my head. "I don't want to deplete our supplies for Epo-5. I can just take a standard—"

But Chambers shoved the water bottle toward me and shook his head. "Your body needs it. Take it."

<Do it.> Cain's tone left no room for argument in those two words.

I threw Cain a disgusted look but took the bottle.

"Confirming we are going to Rockerton's," Ochoa said.

"Yes." *<On that, I won't take no for an answer.>* I threw my next words at Cain. "It was only a nightmare. I'm fine."

Cain studied me, and I caught the glimmer of uncer-tainty in his eyes. I appreciated the concern but didn't want to dwell on it. The experience was embarrassing. Here I was, supposed to be the bad-ass woman going to stop Lucas and beat Yilmaz and Dr. Ashter to the prize of Epo-5. No one had said those words out loud, but I knew that was the hope on every crew member's face I'd passed before we'd left the *Samaritan*.

<There's nothing to be embarrassed about. We all deal with our demons in different ways. Consciously and subconsciously.>

<I don't need a therapy session. Thanks.>

Cain scowled but didn't press. I shouldn't have snapped, but I didn't need a reminder of my weaknesses. I couldn't afford a mental breakdown or anything that might slow me down. I was Mahia Orion. I was done being shoved and pushed around. So I wasn't particularly happy when my mind played tricks on itself.

"This is the shuttle *Scout X-13* requesting permission to dock," Ochoa said.

After a few tries, a static-filled response came. "This is Rockerton's, the rockin' rock of the vast emptiness. Stake your claim and claim your steak."

Ochoa snorted in a thinly veiled attempt to not laugh. "We need one docking space for two hours. Looking for quick turnaround with supplies."

"No worries at all, *Scout X-13*. We'll slot you into a nice and cozy docking ring, Level 23, Berth 31A. Need a wax and shine while you're here? Only costs a few extra credits. Or how about a good old-fashioned bug hunt? We can clear out any vermin hitchhikers in a nanosecond with Exeter's Extermination. They're on sale this week."

"A wax and shine sounds good. Come with a full-polish package? I could use a bit of extra detailing," Ochoa responded.

I frowned and gave Cain a puzzled look. "What's she on—"

He shushed me, so I sulked.

"You betcha. Need some buffing done? We can add that too. A full polish with a buff will set you back… seven hundred and thirty-seven credits. Direct or transfer streams?"

"Direct. Paid on entry," Ochoa confirmed.

"Okey dokey, *Scout X-13*. We'll have you shined up and ready to roll with your time slot. Thanks for doing business at Rockerton's." The real-life voice cut out, and a recording with a slightly bored voice started up with a full list of discounts and all the on-sale gadgets, services, and goods anyone could dream of.

"Now can I ask?" I asked.

"Sure," Ochoa replied.

"What in the worlds are you paying for?"

Ochoa twisted in her chair and grinned. "An extra layer of protection. You don't think I really care about how the shuttle looks, do you? A full-polish package will ensure complete privacy, and the buff will have an encrypt team double-check our systems, make sure there isn't anything lurking around in our coding."

"Oh. Well, then."

"Rockerton's is used to dealing with IGJ and other organizations using their services but needing to keep everything discreet. It's how they stay in business. And why they're not tethered to a specific locale. Can't claim loyalties that way," Cain explained. "Those who've been invited to do business know their unique locator codes and can find them when needed."

I should've suspected a reason everyone was okay with taking the risk of transferring data packets at a place like Rockerton's.

"Any other tidbits I should know?" I asked.

"No. Not for now. Only if Aj-Otha and I aren't back when the two hours are up, Chambers has orders to high-tail it out of there," Ochoa said, as calm as a cucumber.

I really didn't know why that expression ever became a thing, but I remembered Pops loved using it.

And I wished I felt the same.

3

Eeny, Meeny, Miny, Moe

I know what I was expecting—the two hours to be up, with Ochoa and Aj-Otha not yet returned. One thing I'd learned over the past couple of months was that plans didn't ever go as I hoped.

But lo and behold, the universe took pity on us, and the two returned with three minutes to spare.

"We need to go. Now," Ochoa snapped, looking hassled.

"All warmed up for you," Chambers replied. He slipped out of the chair and tucked himself into his little corner of the floor.

"Report," Cain said with a tail wiggle despite the cramped space. Emotions rushed through our telepathic connection—concern, alertness, frustration, and disgust. "Pardon me," he added through gritted teeth. "Old habits and such."

"No apologies needed," Ochoa replied. "I appreciate the training you've had, since we're headed into a hostile situation."

"Rockerton's, this is *Scout X-13*. Requesting release immediately."

A reply came promptly. "*Scout X-13*, we read you loud and clear. All units stand by. Docking disengagement begun. Stand by in three… two… one. And released."

"Easing out in three… two… one. Prepping overdrive engines. Thanks, Rocky. See you next time."

"Take care, Rosa."

I looked at Cain. <*Rosa?*>

He shrugged. That wasn't the name in her file. Then again, if Rockerton's was frequented by the IGJ, perhaps it was an alias. Or maybe the name she was using was an alias, and Rosa was her actual name. *In that case… Knock it off. Lio vouched for her.* But after Dr. Ashter's betrayal—who'd been working for Yilmaz all along—not being suspicious was hard.

"So, what's up?" I asked once the coordinates had been input and the shuttle's nav system took over.

Ochoa swiveled the chair around to face us. That wasn't good. She hadn't done that before. Cain and I had to rearrange ourselves in order to make room. But if she needed to look at us directly, then the news certainly wasn't any good. *Can't be worse than what Yilmaz put us through.* Cain nudged me with his shoulder. He was right. We had no time for self-pity.

"There was only one data packet waiting for us. From Miles."

"And that's got you ruffled because…?" I asked.

"I think it's better if you hear it for yourself," Ochoa said. "Go ahead, Aj-Otha."

The message started off with a lot of background

chatter—not interference but literal chatter from a large group of people. The people were unhappy—in fact, downright angry. Someone cleared their throat, then Miles started talking.

"I'm not one to look on the dark side of things, but everything is going from bad to worse to horrific. War is imminent. The Jumjul didn't take kindly to my brother's less-than-stellar response, with everyone pointing fingers at each other over the whole situation with Lucas and his followers. Rumors are flying that the Jumjul are going to break their word—which is virtually unheard of—and declare war on Old Earth itself. Yilmaz has gone radio silent and left some stupid puppet in her wake. So if you didn't feel the need for urgency before, I'm hoping you all have a few smarts left in those lovely heads of yours to understand what's at stake."

A few indecipherable shouts sounded in the background, followed by the unmistakable sounds of weapon fire.

"Is that it? Is he—" I couldn't even say it. Though Miles was a slippery eel at best, I'd grown attached to him.

Ochoa shook her head. "Keep listening."

"Look, kids, I'm all for believing in you guys and finding the you-know-whos, but I've got to tell you… I'm feeling some unnatural stirrings to give my brother a good earful and see what I can do to control the damage he's done. I may be half-mad, but I can't say that I'm thrilled about seeing my home world turned into a pile of rubble. Because there's no way Old Earth is going to hold their own against the Jumjul, and everyone knows it. So, Mahia—I'm taking a gigantic leap of faith here—whatever is going on with you had better have some answers to this whole situation. Because I—"

His voice was cut off by the sound of a thousand different sirens going off at once then ending in a hiss of static. Ochoa held up her hand. "Wait for it."

The static popped a few times, then Miles came back. But his voice sounded unfamiliar, hushed, and low. "Sending coordinates. See you at Epo-5."

Where in the world is he? Or better yet, where does he think the Star Eaters are?

I leaned back against the shuttle's hull and felt a shiver of anticipation and fear run through me. Lucas had certainly kicked the Farle nest by falsely accusing the Jumjul of preparing for military action. They didn't take kindly to lies, especially ones that concerned them. Unfortunately, the rest of the message was the landing coordinates and no other information.

"Proceed?" Aj-Otha asked.

"Yes," I replied. "Where do Miles's coordinates line up with ours?"

We'd spent the first few days of shuttle time working through various aerial maps of Epo-5 to determine where to start. I overlaid the past three survey maps of the planet, along with areas showing where academic research had been conducted. Secretly—or not so secretly, since I was sure Cain knew what I was doing but decided not to comment—I hoped looking at the maps would spark a memory, something to give me a clue where I needed to go and what on Pluto I was supposed to be looking for. Nothing, unfortunately. So I made my best educated guess.

For our primary target, I settled on an old landing base not far from where Pops had worked. But the others agreed Yilmaz would look there too. So we came up with three other potential landing sites short distances away from my original choice but secluded and on the edge of the waste bogs.

"Roughly two hundred kilometers to the east of your original target," Aj-Otha said.

"That's quite a way off from what you were considering," Cain noted. "He hasn't been to Epo-5. Why would he choose those coordinates?"

"A secure landing site to meet up?" Aj-Otha offered.

"Or information passed on from Captain Lio," Ochoa said. "This could be where Lio feels the most comfortable sending a landing party. Once he enters Epo-5 space, he'll be playing tag with Yilmaz."

"No. There's one thing you're all missing," I said. "Miles was to pick up the Star Eaters. If he's sending us coordinates, then I'm betting the information is coming from them."

"And you're sure that's the best course?" Ochoa said.

I nodded. "Yes. We'll follow Miles's play." A small sliver of anxiety disappeared as I felt a renewed sense of purpose. I wasn't the only one working on figuring out what was up with Epo-5. Others held answers and could help me understand.

"Bring up the holo of Epo-5," Cain said.

Chambers pulled his legs back and brought out the portable holobase. The world of Epo-5 sprang to life.

As far as planets went, it wasn't large. In fact, it only missed the whole Pluto debacle by a few kilometers. Epo-5 sported one moon and a debris field believed to be from two other moons. The planet and its neighbor Sicilia Prime were both within the Goldilocks zone for their solar system—a good thing for the two different species that evolved in that system and a bad thing for the original inhabitants of Epo-5, since the Sici ended up using their planet as a dump site for waste fuel before they upgraded to a friendlier energy system.

Despite one of the prevailing theories, that an extra-terrestrial force destroyed the species on Epo-5, all xenologists agreed on one thing: the Sici weren't the bad guys, at least when it came to the destruction of the Epo-5 inhabitants. It was a well-established fact that the Sici lived at an industrial level of civilization when whoever or whatever disliked Epo-5 decimated the planet. But that still left a ton of unanswered questions.

"You had pinned the old landing base for Research Outpost 3." Ochoa leaned forward and touched the corresponding location on the holo. An orange dot appeared, and she moved to mark the spot Miles had indicated—up close and personal with the only moun-tain range on the planet.

"Is there anything around the area that provides a clue as to why this location?" Chambers asked.

Studying the map, I enlarged it and zoomed in to enhance the topography. Research Outpost 3 had been built on a fairly wide plain. Off to the east were

Hermann's Mountains, which gradually angled south, ending at Research Outpost 2. Ruins dominated the area on the east side of the mountain range. That vast area of complex ruins, with academia declaring the area the largest city on Epo-5, was dubbed E-Complex 9. Pops had been assigned to the lesser ruins around Research Outpost 3, W-Complex 5, W-Complex 3, and the W-Anchors C through G. Those had been the focus of the xenologist student's academic papers, which Pops had worked on verifying.

Lucas and I had been free to do as we pleased while on Epo-5—within reason. Several areas were marked off-limits by the Sici oversight committee and the insurance adjusters who'd approved Pops's research ticket. Despite the inoculations and precautions, some areas were deemed too hazardous for exploration. I remembered Pops and a few of his colleagues joking about insurance adjusters and how the red zones were nothing more than the big corporations not wanting to spend anything on hazard pay. But I didn't think we'd ever wandered as far as where Miles was directing us.

My head was aching with all the possibilities and the slew of memories I was trying to dredge up. I stretched, trying to not hit anyone, then rubbed my temples.

<Chambers could help relieve your tension,> Cain suggested.

<No. I want a clear mind for all of this. It's just a little headache is all. It'll go away once I can get up and move around a bit.>

He didn't press the matter and instead asked, "Does anything match up with areas of your father's research?"

"No, I don't think so." I leaned back and sighed. "His papers focused on the ruins around Outpost 2, where he was supposed to reconcile the differences in the students' work. If I remember correctly, he mostly worked in W-Complex 3. But my memory is fuzzy. I'm sure he visited all the surrounding ruins. If there was one thing Pops was known for, that was being thorough."

"Then the question remains, do we follow Miles's coordinates?" Ochoa asked.

"I believe Mahia answered the question. Just not how she thinks she did." Chambers replied. He pointed at the coordinates from Miles. "This is in a red zone. Our suits will provide protection for roughly twenty-four hours, but beyond that, and we're compromised. Radiation sickness will show—nausea, dizziness, diarrhea, vomiting—"

"We get it," Ochoa interrupted. "It won't be pretty."

"So, what? Miles is leading us on a wild goose chase? I highly doubt it. Miles might be a few things, but on this…" I shook my head. "No, there's got to be a reason for the coordinates."

"Fine," Chambers said. "But we shouldn't land in the red zone."

"Agreed." Aj-Otha leaned forward and touched the holo. "You picked this area as another potential landing site. We could adjust south by fifty kilometers. That would put us roughly twenty-five kilometers outside the red zone—a solid three-to-four-hour hike to the edge, where we can scan the area and decide the best course of action. If Miles is meeting us there, then it stands to reason he has equipment to lessen the side effects, and we would be able to safely dampen comms at that range and check in with him. And if he's not there, we wait."

I glanced over at Cain, who nodded in agreement. "Fine. That sounds solid." I stared at the holo. *Miles, you'd better not be up to your games this time. I'm counting on you.*

4

It's Go Time

Once we were within range, Ochoa scanned the area around Outpost 3, our landing target, and Miles's coordinates. Yilmaz and Dr. Ashter appeared to be nowhere in sight, bless Jupiter. When Ochoa widened the scan, we discovered a large encampment clustered around Research Outpost 5—a solid four hundred sixty kilometers to the west of Outpost 3.

"Any guesses why they'd settle there?" Ochoa asked after she relayed the information.

That stumped me. "Outpost 5, the newest of the lot of them, has been the one with relatively little activity. In fact, I think they shut down the area a few years after they constructed the outpost."

"Confirmed," Aj-Otha said. "Built in 2587 and closed in 2590, standard Old Earth. Reasons cited were difficulties with the surrounding waste bogs leaching through to the outpost, lack of supporting artifacts to indicate settlements in the area, and lack of research funding for agricultural or animal husbandry topics."

"Then why waste their time? What would Dr. Ashter know or have access to?" Ochoa asked.

Or what was it within the files I sent from Dar that tripped his alarm bells? Dr. Ashter had played his cards wisely. No one had suspected the devious little man, not even Miles, who was as devious as they came. He could have stayed on the *Samaritan* and watched for my next move. But he'd run back to Yilmaz, and they'd taken off. *So what am I missing?*

"Do we need to consider a different course of action?" Cain asked.

I turned and stared at him with uncertainty. Dr. Ashter was renowned and brilliant and had access to a plethora of information. The odds were that he knew something I didn't. A memory surfaced, of Pops standing at a table of recently unearthed and decontaminated artifacts. He was unhappy, upset about something. I closed my eyes and tried to hold on to the images.

Was Pops arguing with someone? Maybe. My memory certainly constructed his movements that way. Then abruptly, Pops turned around and faced me, his expression thunderous.

My eyes snapped open.

<Mahia?>

"It's nothing," I said, shaking off my insecurity and the dull pounding in my head. "When Lio arrives with backup, we can send a team to investigate Yilmaz and Dr. Ashter. For now, we stick to the plan. Pops never worked at Outpost 5. We need to go where he was and hedge our bets that Miles has gotten a clue from the Star Eaters."

If the others felt differently, they didn't voice their opinions. And Cain stayed oddly quiet, though I could sense his concern. But I needed to stay the course. It wouldn't do me or anyone else any good if I started second-guessing anything. I'd pored over everything I could get my hands on, and my gut was telling me we were headed in the right direction.

The biggest concern, though, was landing without triggering a full-scale assault from the *Justus*. They'd outfitted the *Rapscallion* and its sister ships with cloaking tech. And the *Samaritan* had likewise had that tech added to all of its shuttles. But once we were planetside, the clock started ticking. As hard as we might try, we had no way to completely obscure our presence on the planet. You could bet your shiny rockets that Yilmaz was using every piece of tech available to watch out for us.

Ochoa and Aj-Otha went to work. Our brief excursion to Rockerton's turned out to be well worth the extra credits. The full polish and buff had set up a network of dampening fields and feedback loops, all designed to spoof our signal. While we couldn't fully hide from the *Justus* or whoever else might be lurking, we could at least buy enough time to fool their systems and get where we needed to go.

"Once we land, we gear up and scuttle the shuttle. Clear?" Chambers reiterated for the third time.

I couldn't help but snort a third time either. *"Scuttle the shuttle" indeed.*

"Clear." Undermining our means of getting off the miserable little planet wasn't my first choice. But Ochoa and Aj-Otha had worked on programming the shuttle to take off and land in several random areas, all while mimicking life signs and activity. That plan wouldn't fool Yilmaz for long, but we needed to buy ourselves a little more time. With Miles meeting us there and Lio on his way, we were gambling on being able to have another way off planet. And if that didn't pan out, well, the odds of us surviving the expedition weren't all that great, anyway.

"Landing protocol initiated," Aj-Otha said.

I leaned my head against the wall and closed my eyes. <*What I wouldn't give for another vision from the Third right about now.*>

Cain arched an eyebrow. <*Really?*>

<*Yes, really. You can't tell me they wouldn't know what's up. They were the ones who asked for my help. And they have some kind of connection with this place.*>

Cain didn't respond, which I took as disapproval. *Fine.* The responsibility for everything wasn't resting on his broad shoulders. *Or his well-toned body… or chiseled features… or—*

<*I can hear that, you know.*>

<*Your point being?*>

That earned a soft growl and a dangerous glint of emerald in his eyes. Maybe I was feeling a rush of adrenaline, knowing we were prepping to land, but I so wanted to goad him into action.

"Brace for landing," Ochoa said.

I took a deep breath and had to stop staring at Cain. Then I slowly exhaled. We had no time for any of that. *Focus.* Whatever awaited us on Epo-5, I had to be ready to face it head on. *But can I? We're talking about potentially facing what my pops was really all about.*

<You will. And we will.> Cain's reassurance quelled some of my anxiety but not all.

<Just promise me that, no matter what happens or what we might learn, we'll make it out. Together.>

Cain's hand found mine, and he squeezed. *<No matter what happens.>*

We landed without issues, and as soon as all systems were green, Chambers had us up and getting into our gear. We changed out of the standard issue jumpsuits into heavily modified hazmat suits. There'd been a bit of debate—and by debate, I meant argument—concerning the type of suits we should use. Chambers had argued for something a bit bulkier, which would've been able to provide protection against the harsh terrain we were bound to come up against, plus the radiation.

But Ochoa and the others felt like the added bulk would slow us down too much and voted for the hazmat suits, which Ochoa reasoned were an acceptable risk. They were constructed from a malleable material designed for ease of movement but would still be able to shield us from the radioactive waste outside the red zone for roughly a week without decontamination protocols. I'd hated those as a kid—standing in line, waiting to be scrubbed down and checked out by the doctors.

I hooked up the suit's air-recycling unit and took a deep breath. Chambers double-checked the suit's readout and nodded. "Activate the face shielding, and you're good to go. But remember to be careful. These suits aren't up for rough-and-tumble antics."

The face shields on the suits were an enormous step up from what I'd had to wear as a kid. Constructed out of a flexible material that gently lay along the contours of the face, they felt like a dream—I couldn't feel a thing. In fact, as I moved my mouth and made faces at Cain to check it out, he rolled his eyes.

As Chambers checked the rest of our little crew, he saw me and laughed. "Just remember outside the red zone, the face shielding can be deactivated to drink or eat. But once we're in the red zone, we switch over to nutrient packs."

Chambers gave Aj-Otha the go-ahead to crack open the shuttle. That was like opening a big otula nut—a favorite snack amongst Glipglows—you never knew what you were going to get. It might be rich in flavor or a shriveled, foul-tasting nut. *Who am I kidding? I know what we're going to get—an enormous ball of nastiness.*

Ochoa took point, and Cain slipped in front of me. *<Hey, down in front. No blocking the view.>* I tried to joke.

He gave an annoyed glance over his shoulder. *<You do what you have to in order to stay alive.>*

<Right back at you.>

A wave of hot air rushed through the shuttle, and despite breathing through the air recycler, the stench of Epo-5 was overwhelming, a hideous mishmash of sulfur, rotten fish, and methane. Talk about your instant gag reflex.

Ochoa took a step forward, her weapon held at the ready as she scanned the area. "Clear."

We moved out, and I took a step to the side, tucked up against the shuttle while I took in the view, a soggy, pustule-filled landscape of belching waste bogs. *How in the world had Lucas and I been allowed to wander around while Pops worked?* It was a miracle the two of us were still alive. If the insurance companies had found out—hoo-boy, someone's head would've rolled.

"Ochoa, you need to see this," Aj-Otha called out from inside the shuttle.

I followed her back inside and peered over Aj-Otha's shoulder as he pointed at the display.

"According to the shuttle's scans, the *Justus* hasn't changed course. Or powered up weapons or deployed any auxiliary shuttles. Would they really just let us land and start our own search without interference?"

"Perhaps they've already figured it out and aren't worried about us anymore," I muttered. That was my worst-case scenario nightmare, that we were just too late.

But Ochoa shook her head. "Then why are they still here?"

"Could have found something but need time to decipher or dig it out," Aj-Otha said with a shrug. "But I'm not reading any disturbances that would show a large-scale excavation or evacuation."

"Then we consider it a blessing and move on," Ochoa said. "Get the shuttle ready. You've got two minutes, then we hustle out."

Aj-Otha needed only a minute and thirty seconds. He had the shuttle taking off and set up for its first spoof.

"All right, people, stay alert. Keep your weapons hot," Ochoa ordered. "Cain, take point. Aj-Otha up next, then Mahia, Chambers, and I'll bring up the rear."

And we were off.

Miles had presented me with a gift before we left, wrapped with a bow and everything. It was the latest Vulture tech, a sleek band of metal around my wrist that communicated with a small node tucked behind my left ear. That baby didn't have any time-wasting controls to push. I activated everything through the mental interface. As we started off, the Vulture unfolded, wrapping its frame around my wrist and building the barrel in a little over ten seconds, three times faster than my previous version. *Can't go wrong with Glipglow self-replicating tech.*

<Cool it.> Cain chided me. *<You're going to blow us up.>*

I let out a nervous giggle and tried to relax. *<Perhaps the mental interface wasn't the best option.>*

<You think?> I swore I could hear him rolling his eyes.

But Cain was right. I needed to calm down. Cain was with me, as were three other well-trained soldiers, hand-picked by Lio. I knew why we were there and what the stakes were, and I needed to keep my focus on my end of our little expedition. That meant unwinding and letting the memories flow. Any little detail I could remember might be a tremendous help.

5

Reunions

Two hours into the hike, I'd relaxed considerably. Nothing had popped up out of the ground, and no one had picked up any signs of activity headed our way. In fact, if I could ignore the bog stench, the day was fairly calm and peaceful—if slogging through a wasteland could be considered peaceful. The sun was shining—rather too cheerfully for my tastes— and the heat wafting up from the ground created a sweltering environment. If not for our biosuits, we would've roasted to a crisp. That was another point that had me seriously questioning the sanity of our father for having let us roam around.

"Cain, let's switch off. Aj-Otha, take point, and Chambers, bring up the rear," Ochoa said.

Everyone switched, and Cain moved in front of me. I didn't need our mental connection to read the tension in his body.

<Doing okay?>

His head bobbed up and down, which meant he wasn't, since he didn't respond verbally.

"Mahia, we're about an hour away from the red zone. Anything you need to update us on?" Ochoa asked.

"Not yet."

She didn't press, which I appreciated. Our landing target and subsequent hike were south of W-Complex 5, far enough away that looking north didn't even give the impression of ruins in that direction. And as we moved east toward Hermann's Mountains, nothing in the distance made me recall anything useful. I was just questioning Pops's life choices and wondering how Lucas and I were still alive.

After what felt like eons and only seconds, Aj-Otha raised a hand and signaled for us to halt. He pointed at himself then motioned downward. Ochoa must've responded in the positive behind me because Aj-Otha knelt then crawled forward. He'd stopped us midway up a small mound, the beginning of the foothills nestled up against the mountains. He moved to the crest of the hill and took a few scans. When he finished, he turned and hurried back.

"No signs of life up ahead, sir," he reported. "Scans aren't picking up any shuttles or heat signatures aside from the waste bogs."

"Then we've beat him here?" I asked.

Ochoa turned and stared at the mountains. "Possible. But the data packet was two days old. He should have been here by now."

"Unless…" Chambers muttered.

Ochoa turned and gave him a hard look. "Yes. Unless a thousand normal things that can go wrong traveling through space. Or the handful of things that could go wrong with this mission. The odds were never in our favor."

The way she stared down Chambers had me wondering what their conversations with Lio had been like. Had they volunteered, or had Lio picked them without giving them a choice? *Doesn't matter. Not anymore.*

"Mahia, do you want to proceed, wait, or head for W-Complex 5?" Ochoa asked.

"We've come this far," I said. "Committed our time and resources to this path. Let's see it through."

<You're laying a lot of trust at his feet.>

<Believe me, I know. But I have to believe Miles has come through.>

"We're twenty-one kilometers away from the coordinates," Aj-Otha said.

"Then we take a twenty-minute break before heading out. Chambers, I want you to run diagnostics, double-check suit systems. Once we cross into the red zone, there's no going back," Ochoa said.

The others sat and took sips of water or snacked on their zips. I couldn't, so I paced.

"You're going to wear yourself out," Ochoa commented then took another bite of her zip.

"Or make me insane," Cain muttered.

I scowled at him and didn't stop. And I knew I wouldn't wear myself out. I needed to think, and moving helped. I blamed Pops for that habit. But this time, the pacing didn't help. My mind didn't dredge up any useful information or flash of memory that would help us out. By the time Ochoa stood, stretched, and told everyone to get up, I was even more restless than when we'd started.

<You're putting too much pressure on yourself.>

<Am I?> I shot back. *<Are you the one everyone has trusted on this crazy mission? Are you the one everyone's put their lives on the line for? Because if this doesn't pan out, then what are we doing here? You can't tell me the others won't blame me for wasting their time. Not when the known worlds are falling apart.>*

Cain motioned for me to follow, and we walked away from the group. He reached out and took my hands then knelt forward until his forehead was resting against mine. *<Leadership. Command. These positions come at a price. Sometimes, they are too great a price to pay. And courage to move forward into the unknown doesn't mean the answers will wait for you. Or that your actions will have the outcome you hoped for. But allowing fear to keep you still or stagnant in a particular area of your life or choices isn't the way.>*

I closed my eyes and tried to soak up his words like a triscal sponge—one of the most porous sponges around, very useful if you could stand having your fingers burned off by the acid they produce. Oh, how my fear wanted to dredge up the old Mahia and snap a few cutting remarks and turn away. Cain was right, and I'd allowed fear to control my life for too long. And that fear didn't like the idea I might turn away from using it as a crutch. *<But how do I move forward without fear?>*

<You can't. That's not the point. It's not that we lose fear or never feel it—it's what we do when we experience it. Do we acknowledge it, accept it, then move on? Or allow it to devour us?>

<When did you get so smart?> I teased.

<You can thank my mother for those lessons. But Mahia>—Cain pulled back and tipped my chin up so that I couldn't look away—*<I will follow you wherever you lead. You're my heart's blood. I'll be with you if you need to turn away. If you need to push forward, I will be there with you. If you need to run—and to hell with everything—I'm there with you.>*

I stared at him, and tears ran down my cheeks. Our relationship had shifted after what had happened on Dar, and I knew Cain loved me. But hearing those words—the permission to do whatever *I* needed to do, not for anyone else, along with the offer to stand with me no matter what happened—ripped off the bandage I'd clumsily applied atop the pain of not having support through what had happened with Pops.

Cain wrapped his arms around me and let me cry. I'd thought I'd been ready to deal with whatever I might learn about Pops or Lucas while searching for answers on Epo-5. But I didn't realize that none of that mattered. What was in the past was in the past. I was here for my healing, to let go and move forward, to not be stuck in the fear of what I might discover.

<It won't be easy,> he said as I pulled away.

<I know. But I'm ready.>

"Are we having a little heart-to-heart? And no one invited me?"

I heard the voice just as the sounds of weapons fire filled the air. I froze, and Cain snapped to attention with his weapon drawn. Slowly, I forced myself to turn around.

Lucas was walking toward us, his arms thrown

wide. Behind him, Ochoa and the others were struggling to fight off who I presumed were Lucas's lackeys.

"What, no hug for your little brother?" When I didn't run toward him, he sighed and dropped his arms. "Well, I suppose I shouldn't have expected much. Just a little disappointing. But we've got a schedule to keep, so let's keep this rolling."

He snapped his fingers, and the air shimmered around us. Then two men and a woman materialized. Cain swung his arm, weapon pointed at the man standing next to me, but the woman behind Cain punched him in the side then disarmed him, flipping his gun around and pressing the muzzle against his head.

Everything happened in a blink of an eye, and I tried to react, but I didn't have the training Cain did. I was too slow, and the man grabbed my arms and twisted them behind my back.

"Gentle, Ritter, gentle. Don't damage the goods," Lucas said.

"If you hurt him, I'll—" I started, but Lucas and the others laughed.

"You'll what, sis?" He stopped in front of Cain and reached out to grab his face. Flecks of black appeared in Cain's eyes.

"This is who you choose to slum it with? You could've done better."

"What, like the company you're keeping is stellar?" I snapped. "I think I'll stick with my choices, thank you."

Lucas let go of Cain and turned his attention to me. "We'll see." He turned and moved away, his goons forcing Cain and me to follow.

<Suggestions?> I asked.

<Rip them to shreds.>

I shared the sentiment but sent, *<Not helpful.>*

Ochoa and the others had fared no better than we had. All three were on their knees, their hands behind their heads. The woman forced Cain down into the same position next to Chambers, while my drooling buffoon stopped me in front of the little impromptu gathering. It didn't take a fool to put two and two together.

"How'd you figure out where we'd be?" I asked, the briefest flicker of concern raising its ugly little head. *What if Miles had played us? He's always had his own agenda. That message we received... Could Miles be in on this with Lucas?*

Lucas grinned. "I'm glad to see your time with the half-breed hasn't dulled your wits."

"Just answer the questions, Lucas."

He shrugged. "Pretty easy to deduce, really. I've been keeping my eye on you. Making sure you're staying on track."

"And Miles?"

"The glorious would-be emperor is none the wiser regarding my rather ingenious hack of his message. But don't you worry—he's safe and sound... for now. You've got much bigger glories ahead than getting in bed with the would-be emperor."

The really not-so-kind retort, filled with indelicate words, was right on the tip of my tongue. But I swallowed them and forced myself to relax. *This is classic Lucas, using words to taunt and see what shakes loose. Miles is many things, but he wouldn't betray us like this. I have to believe that.*

"At least he uses real silk sheets," I said.

Lucas laughed. "Nice. All right, back to business. Shall we go around and give updates?" When I remained silent and no one else spoke up, he sighed. "Fine. I'll go first. So, we're proud to announce a new acquisition for the fleet of the Sun Worshipers—not an inventive name, but I can roll with it. Behold"—he flung an arm skyward—"the *Justus*."

"The what now?" I said.

"You didn't think you made it all the way to the planet on your own, did you? Oh, that's sweet. Nope, Yilmaz would have blown you out of the sky if she could. A bit of a fuss bucket, that one, with some misguided ideas about our family. But she and the good doctor are busy with their own problems right now."

Well… fudge nuggets and the entire bag of chips. I didn't know if I preferred a firefight with Yilmaz and going down in battle or standing here and realizing my brother had played me. *Tough choices these days.*

6

The Squabbles

"Look at it this way," Lucas said. "I'm leveling the playing field. Yilmaz doesn't even know the half of it, but unfortunately, she got a head start. So I'm helping you out. She can't call up to her ship for resources, and they can't come down and stop you. You've got free rein to do as you please."

I was still leaning toward choosing Yilmaz. But as much as I was loath to admit it, having Yilmaz cut off from her ship wasn't a bad thing either. *But did it have to be Lucas? Sure would have been a boost if Miles or Lio had pulled it off.* Lucas and his cronies didn't need another powerful ship in their arsenal. Also, not to get lost in a wormhole of desperation, but the implications of this recent development weren't great either. If they could take over the *Justus*, one of the IGJ's most powerful ships, I had to wonder what that meant for the rest of the IGJ fleet. *How was Lucas going to use the ship?* Pretending to be Yilmaz, he could easily issue commands if he hacked into all the security codes. It would be game over.

"So what, you want me to be grateful? Give you a big hug and just play nice?" I asked.

"If it helps, sure. Why not?" he shrugged.

"Yeah, well… fat chance," I muttered. "So now what? What do you want? To gloat?"

"Nope. Here to help you out."

I narrowed my eyes. "Why? What do you want in return? You never did anything out of the goodness of your heart. It was always tit-for-tat with you."

He grinned. "Learned from the best."

"What, Pops?"

"How do you think he got all the best postings? Could work his way up through the ranks when he came from nothing? It wasn't all based on his good breeding. Pops used his head, knew when to speak and whose hand to grease."

"Like you would know," I snapped.

Lucas's face went slack then into a carefully schooled expression of neutrality, a reaction I recognized. That was how Pops kept his cool when talking with someone he vehemently disagreed with. But I remembered those conversations happening over the dates of artifacts or dig assignments.

"All right. Down to business, then. I'm here to facilitate a brief trip down memory lane. I don't know how much you remember of our time here, but there are a few key things you'll need to conjure up if you want to get ahead of Yilmaz. And I expect you to do just that. You've got the last bit of intel I need, and your life will go a lot smoother if you see reason and help your brother out."

"And life would've been easier if you hadn't turned into a grubby little worm," I muttered. "You know, I remember—the games we used to play, how you loved to trick people. Like the time you wanted to sneak into the supplies bunker but didn't have the access codes. So you begged Pops to take you with him the next time he went, wanted to help and be a big boy. But all you wanted were the codes."

Lucas laughed. "But admit it—you enjoyed the iced lollies, didn't you?"

"I might have," I snapped, embarrassed. "But I went and told Pops."

"I know. Why do you think your nav gear malfunctioned the next day, and you ended up in the opposite direction of where you were supposed to go?"

"You sneaky little rat," I said. "That was you?"

Lucas laughed. "That was a hilarious day."

"Depends on your point of view," I said.

"While I need you to conjure up a few memories for me, these aren't the ones I'm looking for," Lucas said. "Is everyone filled in on the history of Epo-5?" he asked, changing the subject.

"And if they aren't?" I asked.

He motioned to the man standing behind Ochoa. "Then they're deadweight."

"We're well versed in the history," Ochoa said. "The team was handpicked for the assignment."

I glanced at her, but her eyes were focused on Lucas.

"Good to know." He stood there, confident, his shoulders thrown back and his hands resting at his sides. He'd always been confident in whatever misadventure he concocted. That was probably the reason he and Pops had butted heads so often. Lucas had always been so sure of himself, rarely wanting to consider another opinion or a new theory that might disprove the old. I never figured out if that was an effort to earn Pops's approval, to show our father how clever he was, or if he truly thought he just knew it all. I was leaning towards arrogance. *That's kind of your style, though, Pops. Weren't you a tad bit arrogant to have gone over to the Eeri and done what you did?*

Children often viewed their parents through rose-colored glasses, and I couldn't help but wonder if I'd really never seen the true Pops. The past couple of months, I'd had to face the fact I'd never truly known my father. And now, watching my brother, I wondered if it was because I'd simply refused to see him for what he'd truly been. *Was Lucas a window into the truth of my father?*

Before I could slide further into that uncomfortable emotional trauma, Cain interrupted my thoughts.

<Perhaps you need to play the game a bit more.>

I didn't like it, but he was right. I wanted to look over at him and make a face, but I didn't. *<Fine, smarty pants.>*

<But perhaps not as antagonistic,> Cain added.

<Are you trying to tell me something?>

<You do have a habit of—>

<I dare you to finish that thought.>

"What happened to you?" I asked, keeping my focus on my brother. It really was a logical question for me to ask. "How does one go from an annoying little brother to a homicidal maniac?" *Whoops, dial it back.* "I mean, why are you doing all of this?"

Lucas ignored my jab and shook his head. "You really don't remember, do you?"

"Remember? What?" I replied. "I remember you walking out on us. Then radio silence after everything went down with Pops. So I built a life without you. You didn't need me, and so I didn't need you. Now you come back into my life after proudly announcing you're the one who's caused so much destruction?"

"I wasn't the one who left. He did. And he left us long before you think he did. No one knew it yet. But I did. I knew."

"Stop. I don't want mumbo-jumbo, Lucas. If you really want my help, then I want straight, honest answers."

"Honesty? Now you want honesty? Where was the honesty when I needed you the most?"

I stared at him. "What?"

He shook his head. "You're just like him, you know. Fantastic at playing the crowd, being whoever they want you to be." He tilted his head and mocked me. "Oh, the poor little lost lamb, the girl everyone abandoned. Look at me. Take pity on me. Boo hoo."

"I don't know what jute-store novels you've been reading, but that sure as hell wasn't me, and you know it."

"Wasn't it, though? How did you end up working for Whimsical Heights before Confore took over? You certainly didn't go in with a skill set the company was looking for."

I grimaced at the accusation. "What would you know?" I all but yelled. "I needed a job, something to keep my mind off the fact our father had been labeled the worst human in history. In *history,* of all things. And where were you? I could have used someone to lean on."

"I was exactly where I needed to be. Away from you. And away from him. Did you really think I'd come crawling back to you after what happened?"

"Lucas, unscramble that disgusting mind of yours. Nothing happened other than you being a complete ass to me as we got older, always pulling stupid pranks and trying to get me in trouble."

"Yeah, well, Daddy's little perfect angel needed a few humbling moments," Lucas snapped.

<This is not helping. I understand your anger, but channel it for a useful—>

<Don't,> I snapped. I didn't care that Cain was right. Lucas had always had a knack for getting under my skin. And I was out of practice at dealing with him.

Lucas turned away from me and motioned to one of his lackeys. They huddled together while I tried to rein in my temper.

<It's worth considering the chance he's had some kind of mental break.>

I wasn't looking for helpful tidbits, but Saturn's rings, Cain had another good point. And that was a possibility I hadn't even considered. *Who knows who or what Lucas has been listening to, where he's been getting his information?* Obviously, it was someone or something pretty nasty, considering what he'd done. But the implication that I'd done something terrible and promptly forgotten about it made me want to punch Lucas in the face even more. *Family.*

7

Family Road Trips

"Ritter, Shelia, get these surplus body bags prepped and ready to go. Thomas will ship out first then send out the okay for the rest of you lot," Lucas ordered.

The man who'd been holding me spun me around and yanked the Vulture off my wrist then reached up and plucked out the command node before I could swat his hands away.

"What are you doing?" I asked. *Dumb question.* But being ambushed by my insane brother was temporarily scrambling my brain.

The man leered at me and leaned forward. In a competition for the most noxious odor, he would have knocked the boots off Epo-5.

"Just checking out the goods," he whispered and pushed himself a tad too close. "Wondering why someone of your status would pollute herself with such gene filth."

I don't think so, buddy. I let him take one more step then kneed him in the groin, stamping down hard on his foot. Even through his suit, I'd made contact. He winced but didn't move away. I tried to punch him in the throat, but his hand shot up and caught my fist.

"Lively, eh?" His grin was as wicked as they came.

"As lively as they come. But you really should pay more attention to your dental hygiene. Don't they have Minty-White Dissolvo Tabs on the *Justus* or whatever hole you slunk out of? They're standard in all aid ration packs," I said, prepared to slam my forehead against his ugly-looking mug.

Then a shot went off.

"Enough. Ritter, I gave you orders, and they didn't concern my sister," Lucas said. He sounded bored, but when I glanced at him, I remembered the man on the *Whimsy* who'd shown me what Lucas had done to him. The memory was a sobering reminder that I was dealing with a lunatic and his pack of insane followers.

Too many seconds after the fact, I realized Ochoa was no longer kneeling next to the others but had crumpled to the ground. "Ochoa!" I tried to wrest myself from Ritter and go to her, but he didn't let go.

I glared at Lucas. "You're as rotten as—"

"Good grief, she's not dead. Not yet, at least," Lucas said as he kicked at Ochoa to get her to roll over. "I'm sure whatever bioupgrades she's sporting will get to work and triage the worst of it." He looked at me then waved his gun at the others. "But I trust you understand the point I'm trying to make. Sometimes, words just aren't enough, it seems. Or do I need to spell it out?"

He calmly moved to stand behind Cain, and the

woman who'd been guarding him stepped to the side. "I can reiterate my point if need be." He pointed the muzzle at the back of Cain's head.

"No," I said. "But you're insane."

"No more than Pops was, I'm afraid." With a shrug, he holstered his gun and glared at his people. "I thought I issued orders."

His faithful nutjobs snapped to attention. They pulled Cain, Chambers, and Aj-Otha to their feet, while Ochoa—not treated with any compassion—was lifted up and supported between two of the men. Thank the universe she wasn't unconscious yet, and I caught her eye. I mouthed "Sorry," but she smiled and gave a slight shake of her head. If we made it out alive, I decided Ochoa was someone I wanted on my trusted friends list. That would put it up to four.

"Ready for the rules?" Lucas asked with a sly smile.

"Rules? Why, so you can change them?" I remembered his stupid rules with the games we played as kids. When he wasn't winning, he changed them. And if I protested, he threw a fit. *Little hope of that personality trait having been eradicated.*

"But isn't that how the real world works? How do you think corporations, governments, or any number of authority-type positions get to where they are now? They set the rules. And they change them as needed in order to maximize profit or whatever outcome they're looking for. You can't blame me for understanding how life works."

"For corrupt people, sure," I said. "But not for decent individuals. Which you clearly grew up not to be."

"But are they, though? Or is that just a word jealous people use to make themselves feel better?" Lucas said with a nasty grin. "So, back to the rules. You help me. Do as I say, and your heart's blood and his companions will live. Ignore me or try to trick me or be your stubborn self, and well, then you need to say goodbye right now."

My eyes found Cain's. <*I don't know if I want to become the person I'll have to be in order to get us out of this.*>

<*You play his game. Do what you need to in order to survive. We all understood the risks when we stepped on that shuttle with you. I promise we'll get through this together.*>

I glanced at Ochoa and the others then turned to look at Cain's amber gaze. <*And they'll die. Because of me. Just like Lucas and his sycophants. Just like my father and all those people on the* Rapscallion. *But I don't want to be like them. I don't want to sacrifice people or throw them away.*>

<*You are not your brother. Ochoa and the others have trained for this. I've trained for this. This is what people do when they are willing to fight for what they believe in. And we believe in you.*>

His words were pretty—eloquent, even—just not what I wanted to hear. I was ready to put my life on the line but wasn't prepared to justify having others do the same, an attitude I should've realized when I'd sent Lio and Miles on their errands. But when we'd been on the *Samaritan*, surrounded by people who believed in justice, in what was right—it was easy, in fact, to make plans, to believe my decisions were the right ones. But seeing Lucas and listening to him unsettled me. His presence forced me to consider the cost of what we were doing.

But I didn't want to show weakness, especially in front of Lucas.

"I'm not saying goodbye." I ground out the words.

"Good. Then you and I are going to take a little trip down memory lane while everyone else gets cozy on the *Justus*. When we're finished with the family reunion—provided I'm satisfied—then everyone's free to go," Lucas said.

"No."

<*Mahia, don't try*—>

Lucas lifted an eyebrow. "Excuse me?"

"I'll help you, but Cain comes with us, and the others stay right here, with Ochoa receiving any medical treatment she needs. I want video confirmation while we're off on our little trip that they're taken care of, not whisked off into nowhere land."

"You're not really in a position to demand things," Lucas said, giving me an appraising look I didn't appreciate.

I stepped forward and stared at him. "But I think I am. You need me. And I'll help you—all the way, whatever it takes—but only under those conditions."

Under any circumstances, I would've wanted to win the stare down, now more than ever. But I made a tactical decision and blinked. *Let him think he can still best me.*

Lucas tilted his head to the side, still holding his unwavering stare, and said, "All right. New orders, then. Call down for support and add in one of the med techs for fun. Shelia, you'll be our spokesperson. We'll check in every hour. But the half-breed stays here. This is a family-only excursion."

"Then I'd say we don't have any time to waste, do

we?" I said, trying not to focus on how much I hated my brother. "Shall we head out?"

Lucas laughed. "Sure. Why not? Pops always did like your go-getter attitude."

<Be careful. Stay safe. And we'll make it through this,> Cain said as Lucas gave me a slight shove to get going.

<Don't worry. We are going to make it out alive. And we'll bring him to justice,> I told Cain as I started walking.

<Keep me updated as much as possible.>

<I will. If you get the chance, show these guys who you really are.>

Even though I was far enough away that I shouldn't have been able to, I could've sworn I heard a rumble of thunder inside his chest. Cain would get free, and I knew the others would do what they could as well. And if the universe was still batting for our side, then Miles and Lio would work through whatever setbacks they'd encountered and be here before we knew it. Then we would kick everyone's butt.

8

Uncomfortable Memories

Lucas and I passed over into the red zone in silence. Cain had tried to soothe my fraying nerves but only succeeded in putting me more on edge, so he went silent too. I wanted to get our misguided family reunion over with, and as I glared at my brother's back, I wished several unforgivable things, and as soon as I mumbled one, I felt a rush of guilt. But the guilt evaporated within the next few steps as a new thought popped up and the cycle repeated itself.

"What would Pops say if he could see you now?" I finally asked, breaking the silence.

We'd been walking for over an hour and had passed our first check-in with Shelia and the gang. The foothills had grown, becoming more rugged, with the mountains gathering in force in front of us.

"You know, I've asked myself that same question for a few years now. And the answer really depends on the time frame you set it in," Lucas answered. "If you were to ask the Pops who worked on Epo-5 that question, I dare say he'd be proud of me—for the initiative I've shown. If you asked the man who ran off to the Eeri, well, he'd be disappointed."

"More like devastated by what you've done," I muttered.

"No. You misunderstood me. Not disappointed because of the steps I've been forced to take but the fact I've been so slow in seeing them through. I really should've reached out to you much sooner, but Mrs. Gol… She had other plans, and I had to tread lightly for a time. The woman might not have accepted what I represented, but… we were working toward the same goal. It's a pity what happened."

I stopped dead in my tracks. "I feel as if I should be shocked. But you know, after everything, I don't think I am." I shrugged and started walking again. "It would make sense one looney would search out another."

"Oh, my dear, misguided sister. There's so much you have yet to learn. And before we reach our designated coordinates, I brought along a few tools to help."

"I don't need to learn anything from you. You don't have anything I want," I said, pushing my way past Lucas.

I didn't need him to guide me. We'd set ourselves up on a straight trajectory toward the coordinates we'd so foolishly believed had come from Miles. And Lucas and his cronies hadn't interfered with my suit's nav systems.

"I'm pretty sure I do. I've got what it's going to take to unlock that tiny little mind of yours, to help you remember what you've walled off."

I spun around and marched up to him. I poked him in the chest. "I haven't forgotten anything. There's no great secret lurking around in here, only your delusions."

Lucas leaned forward and knocked on the side of my head like it was some kind of door. "Oh, but you do. But I don't feel much like spoilers at the moment." He grinned and brushed past me. "Do keep up."

I definitely didn't want Lucas to know, but if there was some kind of dark secret lurking in my mind, I really wanted to know, to rip the bandage clean off, like I was trying to do right then, to be done with this whole mess, not unlike how my foray into waxing had gone. On a whim—a stupid whim—I'd visited the Shops of Yesteryears on Original Luna one time.

They had everything a history buff or a role-playing junkie could want: tech stores, beauty parlors, medical shops, clothing outlets, and restaurants. I'd treated myself and had sprung for a packaged deal at one of the beauty parlors. Everything had gone well until we got to the waxing bit. Let's just say that, afterward, I vowed to never do that again. And right now, I felt as if I was back in that parlor with a well-intentioned woman trying to wax my legs but failing—miserably.

Whatever might lurk in the depths of my mind wasn't surfacing. I would've thought after forming a telepathic connection with Cain and having the Third root around in my head that one of those events would've triggered some alarm bells. *Nope. Nada.*

I had to admit I'd been a daddy's girl. Pops had

been a good father, despite anything else that had happened. *Or so I keep trying to tell myself.*

And I'd wanted to be just like him, to be a xenologist, traveling the stars and uncovering the secrets of the universe, but not to the extent of what Lucas was implying. I'd never been perfect and had gotten into my fair share of trouble with Pops, just like Lucas. But it had never soured my relationship with our father like it had him. I hated to even consider it, but maybe in some twisted way, Lucas had a point. Through some distorted lens, he could have believed Pops favored me more than him. And that could have warped his reality into a festering distortion of what our childhood had actually been like.

Fine, I can play along with that. As long as it gets him to open up.

"So what if I was Daddy's little angel? I knew how to play the game with him, get what I wanted. It was better than what you did, always pushing at him, picking at him," I said. *Half truth, half… hopeful lies.*

"The man needed someone to keep him in line," Lucas said.

I couldn't help myself and laughed. "Excuse me? You were a little kid. You didn't leave until you were, what, thirteen… fourteen? How were you supposed to keep him in check?"

"Fifteen. I left when I turned fifteen. Old enough to qualify for an apprentice license as a pilot on short-haul freighters. And if you'd kept a clear head, maybe you would've noticed what was going on: all the late-night meetings, the blocked transmissions and restricted access."

"Pops had a lot on his plate. He had reports to file, government agencies to keep up to date, not to mention staying on top of any teams he managed," I snapped.

"Don't tell me you haven't made the connections yet," Lucas said. "Come on, sis, keep up. We both know what he was involved in."

I opened my mouth to say something I surely would've regretted but snapped it shut. Lucas was right. "Fine. I can admit that. I know he was working for Mrs. Gol and her group."

"Ah, semantics correction. He wasn't working *for*. He was working *with*. An integral part of their group, if I might add," Lucas said.

I ground my teeth. "Working *with*. But it would appear he reconsidered at the end."

Lucas stopped and grinned. "But did he? I think that's a question well worth exploring."

"I don't see how that's a question at all. Pops killed all those people on the *Rapscallion*. To stop the work with the smart-bots. So that Mrs. Gol and her group couldn't have access to—" I stopped. *Does Lucas know about the Third?* I assumed he did, but he'd never said it out loud. "I don't even know anymore," I said, trying to cover my tracks.

If Lucas noticed, he didn't let on. "Come on, sis, aren't you even going to try? If not for me, then for you. Don't you want to understand? To remember the truth of about Pops? And this place?"

"I still don't know what it is you think I'm supposed

to share," I snapped. "This is insane. Even for you. I don't have a clue what you think is going to happen. If you think there's some repressed memory…" *Game time*. "We came here, didn't we?"

"A little obvious."

"No. I mean the two of us. Here. To this forsaken patch of wasteland. We were… what, exploring?"

"I think you can do better than that," Lucas said.

"I'm trying, all right? Help me out, here. We explored that day. Like we usually did when Pops didn't have any lessons for us. We'd been messing around, trying to see who could breathe the longest without the air recyclers. I don't think Pops had figured it out yet, right?"

"Perhaps."

Insufferable piece of junk. "We were looking for ruins. Something to show Pops. Or rather, you wanted to show him. Make him proud of you. But…" I stopped, hoping Lucas might fill in some blanks. He didn't. "We were young. Stupidly young. I don't know why Pops even let us wander around on our own. Pretty poor parenting, considering the health hazards of this place."

"You're forgetting how he kept track of us, though. Remember your brief excursion over the tattoo? How you were so furious he'd kept the tracker on you even after you thought you were all grown up?"

"Yeah, but still… letting little kids play in the waste bogs?"

"Survival of the fittest. Or perhaps he was using us. Wondering what would happen," Lucas said.

I stared at my brother. "What in the worlds are you alluding to? That we were... what, an experiment? Wrapped up in what he was doing with the crazies? I think you're forgetting something, though. He married our mother, someone outside of the breeding fanatics."

"True. But I think you'll find he did so for a very specific purpose. Our father was clever. He knew the breeding program wasn't working, and he needed to try something different, to introduce a different bloodline. But everyone else was so wrapped up in their dogma about who was and wasn't acceptable, they couldn't see the answers staring them in the face."

Uh-uh. No way. "No. I don't believe it," I snapped. "There's no way. Pops wouldn't have done that to us. He loved us. And he stopped the program. He went over to the Eeri in order to make sure the research stopped."

"Did he? Or did he simply wipe out the competition?"

What in the Black Gates of Objer does he mean? Wipe out the competition? His words threw me for a loop.

"What would you know?" I asked, more a rhetorical question than something I truly wanted Lucas to answer. I hadn't considered that angle. Nor did I want to. All the emotional energy I'd spent on working through what I'd learned on the *Rapscallion*—trying to reconcile a man's actions with the father I'd known and loved—flew into the maw of a big, black hole.

"Quite a bit, it turns out. But right now, you need

to stay focused. I'll admit our little chats are fun, but ticktock, little mudsock."

"That doesn't even make sense," I snapped.

"But at least it rhymes."

If the others' lives hadn't been on the line, I would've sat down in the muck, crossed my arms, and refused to play his game. But if I did that, we would all die. *Hell, I think we're going to anyway.*

"Lucas, I don't remember anything strange or horrible happening. We were two kids, allowed to do as we pleased. We got into mischief—trouble, even—and you enjoyed playing tricks on me. You're remembering wrong in that twisted mind of yours," I said.

"Nice try, sis. But I know it's in there somewhere."

<*What in Saturn's rings am I supposed to do? I should have put my foot down with Lio. I should never have agreed to having anyone else come with us. Even you.*> I wasn't sure how far my connection to Cain would last, but I was grateful to hear him, even if it felt distant.

<*You're not alone anymore. This is how relationships work.*>

Teamwork was something I wasn't really familiar with. Sure, while working at Confore, I'd had the weekly meetings and checked in with immediate supervisors, but working the help desk was a lone-wolf type of job. I kept to my callers, and my colleagues stuck to theirs. If questions came up that I couldn't answer, the Confore database was the next step, and if that exhaustive collection of tech manuals didn't do the trick, the caller got passed on to a supervisor for a complimentary coupon offer. Time was money. Another caller was always there for me to try to help.

We fell back into an uncomfortable silence. Well, I was uncomfortable. I think Lucas was reveling in everything—gloating, really.

This really isn't a good day at all.

"Break time," Lucas said cheerfully as he stopped. He walked over, kicked at a sizable rock, and, when it didn't crumble, sat down. "Since you're having a bit of difficulty, and we're on the clock, I think it's time for our first trip down memory lane."

I really didn't like the sound of that.

9

Marriage, Families, and Children

I sat down opposite him. "Got anything to drink?"

Lucas tossed me a water-based nutrient pack, and I hooked it into my suit. The biosuit was a wonder at conserving the body's moisture, but the combination of having a one-on-one with my errant brother, hiking through a radioactive wasteland, and doom pressing down all around had made me a tad bit thirsty.

"Pops's journals," Lucas said as he leaned over and set his pack by his feet. "Really quite fascinating."

"I've read through everything I could get my hands on," I said and unhooked the nutrient pack as the suit finished cycling through it. I tossed the used pack over my shoulder and keyed in the codes for the suit's feeding tube.

The grin on Lucas's face made me choke. I coughed a few times and, when I could speak, asked, "What's that look for?"

He reached into one of his pockets and pulled out

a thin metal chain. The silver glinted in the sunlight, and I froze. *Pops's necklace.* Lucas shifted his weight, and the pendant swayed back and forth. Its amber interior glowed. I stood and closed the distance between us, snatching the necklace from Lucas.

"How did you get it?" I asked.

"How do you think?"

I hissed at him and moved back to where I'd been sitting. Pops had worn the pendant for as long as I could remember. When I was little, I'd tried to sneak up on him and pull it up out of his shirt. It had fascinated me. The amber had been shaped into a perfect oval, with delicate silver filigree around the edges. I would giggle and reach up to touch it. Normally, when I had played my games with Pops and his necklace, he would bat my hands away and tell me either he was too busy to play or it wasn't nice trying to take something that didn't belong to me. His refusal to let me see or play with the pendant had only fueled my curiosity until one night when he was cross about something to do with work—or so I presumed—he snapped and actually slapped my hand away, telling me in no uncertain terms I was to leave his necklace alone. I hadn't tried again after that.

One night, when I wasn't feeling good and was forced to hole up in a medical bay, Pops had stayed with me and read a few stories. I distinctly remembered Pops turning off the small palm pad and leaning over to kiss me goodnight, and the pendant fell out of his shirt and touched my cheek. I stayed still but watched the pendant sway as it dangled from his neck.

Pops sat back down and took the necklace off. He

handed me the pendant, and at first, I refused, but Pops smiled and told me it was all right.

I held it like it was the most precious thing in the known worlds. Pops then told me one last story, of how the pendant had been a gift from when he married.

<Mahia, what's wrong? Are you okay?> Cain's voice felt distant, but it was loud enough to break my concentration.

I jerked in surprise and looked up at Lucas. The little bugger must have been watching me. *<I'm fine. Just… family junk, that's all.>*

"What did he tell you?" Lucas asked.

For a split second, I feared Lucas knew Cain had reached out. But when his eyes flickered to the pendant, I realized what he meant.

"That it'd been a gift when he'd married Mom. That's why he always wore it." I rubbed my thumb over the amber's surface. "Did he ever talk to you about her much?" The question slipped out before I could stop myself, but there it was.

I expected Lucas's face to darken or for him to clam up. Our mom was a tough subject for him.

"No. Not really," he said. But his voice was soft, a hint of raw emotion detectable in his words.

"Me neither. Just those few times he'd get really nostalgic," I said.

"You mean when he had a little too much to drink?" he scoffed.

I frowned and tightened my hand around the pendant. "Whatever."

Lucas leaned forward and held out his hand. I didn't want to give it back, but under the circumstances, I didn't have a choice. He took the necklace and held it up to watch the pendant move back and forth, as if he was trying to hypnotize himself. I almost wished he would've. Then maybe I could've gotten some answers out of him.

"Do you know where it comes from?"

"No, just what I told you. It was a gift."

Lucas reached into another pocket with his free hand and pulled out another necklace, with a pendant exactly like the other.

"You copied it?" I asked.

He shook his head. "No. Mine was also a gift." He held his aloft with Pops's. "A gift from our good friend, Mrs. Gol."

I groaned. "You know, I'd really hoped to be done with that crazy old lady."

Lucas threw me a look of disapproval. "She wasn't crazy. Or at least not until the very end."

"Yeah, whatever you say. You're not exactly a shining example of sanity yourself, you know."

He chuckled. "Each member of the administration circle within the so aptly named Sun Worshipers are given a pendant exactly like this on the day of their marriage—a reminder of why we are dedicated to doing what we do."

"First, I'd really like to know what that is, exactly. But second, you got married?"

He lowered his hands and turned to study the mountains. "Yes. A little over three years ago. Azarin was five years younger and a strong genetic match for the program. Our children would have been among the first to help replace the caliber of individuals Pops so pathetically murdered. Mrs. Gol had been quite vocal about my presence within the group, but she couldn't argue with what the scientists were telling her. Wats Hawking Orion's bloodline needed to be continued—to be purified, of sorts, since all other avenues hadn't been as forthcoming as they'd hoped."

In a few sentences, Lucas had dropped more than a few bombshells.

"Children?" Out of all the potential futures I could've dreamed up, Lucas having children wasn't one of them. And seeing him then, I couldn't even imagine him as a father.

"Two. A boy and girl. Fitting, I suppose." He turned back to face me. "But dead. They're all dead now. Because of Pops, all our work had to be sped up to meet the deadline. And unfortunately, introducing the smart-bots caused rapid cellular decay. Hazel died within two weeks, and Adam"—Lucas's gaze dropped—"within five days. Azarin didn't take the news well. She might have been a strong genetic match, but mentally… She and her family had been with the program for only two generations. They weren't ready to handle the tremendous amount of sacrifice required."

"I'm so sorry, Lucas. I can't even imagine what that must have been like," I said. And I tried to mean every word because even though he had done monstrous things, that didn't mean I couldn't show compassion over such a personal loss. But a voice inside my head whispered, *But he offered up his own children. Why should you feel pity for someone like him?* It was a fair question. But those children would have been my niece and nephew, family I'd never had the chance to meet.

"When did you…" I started to ask. "I mean, how long ago did that happen?" Perhaps that was a little indelicate, but I wanted to know.

Lucas shrugged, but he swallowed hard. "Four months."

I hadn't expected that and wasn't sure how to respond. Four months before, Lucas had had a family. *Were their deaths a catalyst for his psychotic behavior? Did it matter? He was still a mass murderer.*

"Did you never wonder why Mrs. Gol choose the timing she did to come after you? The events with Pops on the *Rapscallion* were several years ago. She'd had time to mourn her son, to move forward," Lucas commented.

That was too much. I had to stand up and move around. "You're telling me the death of your children started all of this?"

"Not started—ended," Lucas said. "Pops messed everything up, but with our children, we had hopes we could rectify the situation, catch up to where we needed—" When a hiss and a pop sounded, Lucas held up a hand. "Hold on a minute."

Shelia's voice came over the comms. "Everything is still quiet, boss. You? Any progress?"

"Negative. Mahia, anything you want to ask?" Lucas asked.

"How's Ochoa?" Because we were still close enough, I knew Cain was seething with frustration but physically all right.

Lucas relayed the question, and Shelia laughed. "As

well as can be. We've patched her up, but if you guys don't hurry, she might not pull through. I'd say she needs a top-notch surgeon."

"Ideally, I'll have a progress update at our next check-in," Lucas said and signed off.

He stood, stretched, then tossed Pops's pendant toward me. I stumbled forward, and my fingers snagged the necklace.

"Hang on to that. Might help unlock some of those memories we need," Lucas said. He checked his nav panel. "Looks like we've got roughly an hour and a half to go before we reach our destination. So I need you to get cracking."

"Even with everything you've told me, I still don't know what you're expecting from me," I said.

He let out a long sigh. "I know, sis, I know. But with what's up ahead, I'm hoping that's all about to change."

10

Nightmares and Memories

I fiddled with the pendant, my thoughts crowded with questions. The least of those was whether I would ever be truly done with Mrs. Gol or if the woman had concocted some haunting story line of revenge. The terrain changed from the swampy death traps of bog slime to equally unpleasant dubious-looking rocks. Whatever chemicals the Sici had dumped on Epo-5, the potent mixture eventually leached into the rocks, and with one touch, they would break open to reveal flesh-eating goo inside, not unlike an old, old treat on Old Earth that had something to do with chocolate and egg-laying rabbits.

Needing to concentrate, I tucked the pendant into one of my pockets. *I know what these foul rocks remind me of. Lava cakes.* And just like that, one of my favorite desserts was off the menu.

<Even though they're chocolate?> Cain asked.

Thank the universe for our telepathic link. He was helping to keep me sane on that stupid family hike. When Lucas and I decided to give each other the silent treatment, Cain helped pass the time. But his voice was increasingly becoming a whisper. And despite all the ideas we'd batted around, neither one of us had a great opening to gain the upper hand over our captors.

That's not quite true—Cain was spitting mad. He just wanted to go for it and let the chips fall where they may, but I told him to wait. Something would happen, and we would get our chance. If nothing else, I had to believe Miles or Lio could show up at any minute.

<I can barely hear you now. What happens when we're too far apart? Will we begin to feel the effects, like what was alluded to in that tale about Itheron and Lia?>

<I don't know. Just focus on finding a way to stay ahead of Lucas. I'll find you.>

I wished I had his confidence. *<You'd better.>*

I wanted to believe him. I forced myself to try to believe him. *Perhaps I shouldn't have told the universe I was done being kicked around, because it sure feels like I'm the butt of a big joke again.* And I'd thought the universe and I had become pals after that helping hand on Dar. *How foolish of me.*

We all passed the next check-in with nothing to report, but as Lucas and I closed in on the coordinates, though I was loath to admit it, something was eerily familiar about the area. Our climb had moved us up in elevation, but we were still only nestled at the base of Hermann's Mountains. Still, the vantage point gave me a pretty good bird's-eye view of the valley. If I'd sported the Hunter's Ultimate Ocular Package in bioupgrades, I certainly could've seen all the way to the third research outpost.

"Are we there yet?" I asked in my whiniest voice.

As I stopped to catch my breath, I knew Lucas had been right. I'd been there before. I just didn't know why. The area hadn't been a part of Pops's research, and while Lucas and I had roamed far afield in our misadventures, I never would've imagined we'd have gone that far. We were a solid four hours into the red zone.

"Here, knock yourself out," Lucas said and tossed me a nutrient pack.

I wasn't liking all these handouts, but turning it down would've been foolish, so I hooked it into my suit. "Tell me. Do you really believe in all the purity crap, or is it just a means to an end for you?"

Lucas was hooking up his own nutrient pack and fiddling with his suit. "Both. Humanity deserves to be at the top, and all this intermingling with other species has corrupted us. Made us soft. Did you know that we're no longer actively exploring? That the Eeri and the Jumjul are the only two species left who are? And I can assure you they're not messing around with new tech in that area either. Talk about shortsighted. We should be out there, on the forefront, making sure humanity has the first rights to new discoveries."

"Soft? Humanity? We've expanded into fifteen different solar systems. Established major trade routes along the way. Helped bring about numerous peace treaties. Humanity was key in establishing the Inter-Galactic Justice system, and before the Cricade Wars, we inhabited the first several worlds looked to for aid and support."

"Glory days of a time long since past," Lucas said with

a shake of his head. "Our military has grown stagnant, and the InterGalactic Justice system is a joke."

"You're wrong. Our alliances with other worlds have only made us stronger. Our beliefs have expanded into new branches of philosophy, religious studies, science, and even our perception of reality. We've made huge scientific breakthroughs because of our collaborations. Sure, we're not perfect—no species is—but we're stronger than we ever were before. Isolation and purity mumbo-jumbo will only drag us down, bring us back into the Dark Ages."

After a pause, Lucas shrugged. "I wouldn't expect someone like you to understand. At least not now, anyway. Although I had hoped I'd be able to change your mind, I can clearly see that's not possible, given your current circumstance."

I glared at him. "What's that supposed to mean?"

"The gene filth you've taken up with?"

I promptly marched over to my brother and slapped him. "Don't ever say that again."

Lucas grinned. "If you behave."

"You disgust me, and I wish you weren't my brother!" I shouted and turned away.

Fury drove me forward and made me clumsy. My foot slipped, the landscape tilted, and my hands shot out to try to catch myself. But my right hand hit one of those disgusting rocks and sank into the horrid, foul-smelling liquid. I tried to yank my hand out of the mess, but the liquid was thick, and I continued to sink until it was halfway up my forearm.

"Stop struggling," Lucas said as he squatted next to me. "Just relax. Wiggle your fingers a bit, and very slowly pull your arm up."

I did as he said and eventually felt my hand move. But Chambers's warning rang through my head with a nasty I-told-you-so lilt to it. By the time my fingers slipped free of the slime, my suit's integrity had been compromised. Black dots swam before my eyes, and Lucas grabbed my shoulder to pull me back. He washed me off, said something about fast-acting acids, and gave me an injection.

And blast the luck of Pluto, a memory bubbled up to the surface.

The day had been warm, too warm for even Epo-5's summer season. The air-conditioning units had been overworked for the past several weeks, and the techs were scrambling to keep up with the repairs. Because of the heat, everyone was ordered to stay inside, and being little kids, Lucas and I quickly got bored. At first, Pops tried to give us assignments, but that was just busywork. When that didn't pan out, he let us come into his workshop and watch him.

I was seven at the time and all grown up. I was much too mature for my little brother and, of course, deserved the coveted seat next to Pops. He was working on analyzing a piece of pottery. Pops explained each step to us, but I kept scooting closer and leaning forward to keep Lucas out of the limelight.

When Lucas had had enough of being left out, he threw a temper tantrum, as little kids were prone to do. And that one was a doozy. He flailed about, wailing and crying, and at one point tripped over a crate and smashed into the table. One of the artifacts Pops had been working on wobbled, and before anyone could react, it crashed to the floor.

I really believe that, if not for the ungodly heat, Pops wouldn't have reacted so drastically. But we were all on edge, kids and adults alike. Pops lost it, marched us both out of the workshop, and ordered us to go to our rooms.

I, of course, placed all the blame on Lucas, and as we slunk down the hall, I whispered to him, "I wish you'd never been born, and so does Pops."

Lucas had turned to stare at me, his already tear-stained face growing puffy, but the look of absolute dejection in his eyes would haunt me. I knew I was in the wrong—I should never have said it—and I tried to apologize after I'd lain down and had a good cry myself. But Lucas hadn't opened his door, and my guilt had eaten away at me.

I blinked and shook my head to clear my mind. Lucas had cleaned off my hand and was squatting off to one side, watching me.

"I remember," I whispered, "that day we were out here, and I said how I wished you'd never been born. That was a pretty rotten thing to tell you." A nasty thought reared its ugly head. *Would Lucas have turned out to be a better person if I'd been a better big sister?*

Lucas nodded. "It was. But we were kids, and I don't blame you. Even then, I knew what had happened to Mom. You know, I would catch Pops at times staring at me, this really horribly sad look on his face. Then, when he would realize I was watching him, he'd grin and always do something silly to cheer me up. Rather, I think it was more to cheer him up than me. Sentimental fool."

"He wasn't a fool," I snapped.

"In many ways, he was. But more importantly, do you remember what happened after you said those things?"

Even if Lucas hadn't turned into a complete psychopath forcing me to walk down memory lane, I still wouldn't have wanted to remember. I tried, but everything was fuzzy after that. I thought I'd stormed back into my room, furious at Lucas again for making me feel so horrible, then lain down on my bed and cried—again. I remembered picturing Pops's face when Lucas would tattle and tell him what I'd said. And if I'd felt bad about how I'd wounded Lucas, then it was a hundred times worse to consider how disappointed Pops would be in me.

"It was so damned hot even my memories melted into a blur," I tried to joke, not really for Lucas's benefit but my own. Even at the moment, with what he'd become, I still hated how hurt he'd looked.

"You ran off. As far as you could get."

Ran off? I certainly didn't remember anything like that. I was just lying in my bed, afraid of Pops's disappointment, and sweltering in the heat. I glanced down at my hand. Lucas had cleaned off all the goo, but the suit had been compromised, and I would need to be extra careful from there on out.

<Close call. We've got to figure out how to wrap this up.> When I didn't hear a response from Cain, I let out a long sigh. *Guess that means we're out of range now.*

"So, if I ran off, then where'd I go? 'Cause I don't

remember that, and I really think I would. What was it, the rec center or something?" I asked, recalling that when we hadn't been exploring, we'd whittled away hours at that center. "What was the woman's name? Kettle? Nettle?"

"Silvia Bettle," Lucas said. "You know, I think she had a crush on Pops. She never let the other kids get away with what we did. Or let them stay in the rec center past hours."

"I'd forgotten that." She'd been around Pops's age, if I recalled correctly. Mild-mannered but smart—spooky smart. "Didn't she double as the administrative liaison or something like that?"

"Yup. And if you ask me, I think Pops played into that little crush. Great way to make sure he got all the supplies he needed."

"That's a little sexist," I said and took a step back.

He stood and shrugged. "We do what we have to in order to survive."

I really hated to admit it, but Lucas had hooked my curiosity. I wanted to know what he was on about with Pops, of course, but telling me I'd run away, when I couldn't remember anything about that, annoyed me. *Dammit.*

I unhooked the nutrient packet, and we continued climbing. The rocks were getting bigger, and eventually, we got to a point where our way forward was blocked by a row of large, unscalable—even if they turned out to be solid—boulders. Lucas gently tapped each one, double-checking, then, apparently satisfied with their integrity, he squeezed between them. I could've turned and run, but instead—like a fool—I followed him through to the other side. And I froze.

I remembered the place.

Three gigantic slabs of rock rose up from the ground. Each one tilted back slightly, and not only did each have dozens of geometrical shapes carved into it, but the shape of each rock had been purposefully crafted into a rudimentary triangle. I had no doubt the carvings were primitive incarnations of the markings found throughout the ruins, and they matched what I'd witnessed from the Third. When I stepped closer, I realized each slab of rock had only one particular geometrical carving— just repeated hundreds of times. But none of the three shapes felt familiar. Nor did seeing so many of one shape clustered together. *I don't recall anything like this from Dar.* Of course, I hadn't had all the time in the world to do a thorough survey. I'd captured what I could, which certainly wasn't all of it.

"This place should have been my memory, not yours," Lucas said as he set the pack down. "Pops knew I carried a higher potential than you did."

"That doesn't make any sense," I said.

Lucas sneered. "Don't you want to know why I tormented you all those years? Why I butted heads with Pops at every turn? Come on, Mahia. I think you're just trying to ignore the truth of who and what you are: a self-centered little brat."

I honestly couldn't say why that particular insult stung. But it did. Without really thinking it through, I launched myself at him. We wrestled, and I tried to snag the gun holstered at his hip. Lucas's response showed he'd spent time training. He was agile, fast, and powerful. Before long, he had me pinned to the ground.

"I've been more than patient with you, sis. But now, you're just wasting my time." He opened up comms. "Shelia. Pick one."

"No, you can't!" I struggled, trying to lift a leg to kick at him, knee him, or anything to unbalance the monster holding me down.

"Got the perfect one, boss." Shelia's voice came through loud and clear.

Then without any other preamble, a gunshot sounded.

Lucas grinned. "Thanks. Check-ins are officially canceled. Wait for further orders."

"I take back any remorse I might've had," I hissed. "I really wish you had never been born. You're a monster."

His grin widened, and he leaned forward. "No more than what you—"

With all of my rage and fury, I slammed my head into his, which gave me the split second of surprise I needed as his grip loosened. I tried to get away, but he snarled and punched me in the gut with enough force to leave me breathless.

"Nice try. But you're not going to get off quite so easy." He hauled me to my feet. He took out his gun and pointed it at me. "Now. Don't worry, I'm not looking to kill you at this point. Maybe a few well-placed shots to make you a little more compliant if need be. But you've still got some memories to share."

"Why in the worlds do you think I'd help you?" I snapped, still feeling the pain in my gut. *<Cain? Can you*

hear me? Please. If you can, try to respond.> I couldn't think
the worst. We were merely out of range. That was all.
Lucas would be a fool to let them shoot Cain, who was
the one piece of leverage he could play. *But maybe he's
counting on me thinking that. Going to dangle the idea of hope
in front of me to get me to do whatever he wants.* A dangerous
game, but he was insane.

<Cain?> I tried again and again until I felt a flicker
of something warm spread through me, and like a fool,
I remembered how hopeless I'd felt on Lunar 5 when
Cain had disappeared and the IGJ had administered the
loprizamine to destroy our connection. I didn't feel that
way now, and realizing that, I relaxed. I had to figure
out how to stop Lucas.

"Fine. Tell me what I'm supposed to remember, and
let's get this over with," I said and turned around—partly
out of bravado, to show Lucas I wasn't afraid of him,
and partly to try to come up with a plan without giving
anything away.

"So, I ran away. To here, I presume?"

"Correct."

"And what…?" *What did he say?* "This should have
been your memory? Why? Because you'd found it first?"
I shook my head. "No, that's unlikely. We always did
stuff together. So why your memory?"

I stared up at the glyphs carved into the rock and
wondered who'd made them. The academics would vote
for the indigenous population, but I wondered if the
Third could have done it. *I wonder if this is all that's left.
When the radioactive material corrupts the stone, what else does
it corrupt? How much knowledge or different clues have been lost*

because of the waste bogs? Could that all play a part into what happened to the Third?

I raised my hand to study where the slime had eaten through the top layer of my suit. *Would the Third be susceptible to radioactive material?* I was beginning to wander down a wormhole. *Stay on—*

"You followed me. That's it." I turned back to stare at Lucas. "I sneaked out of our unit and started walking." Flashes of the day started to come to me. "I had no idea what I was doing. Didn't take any supplies—other than putting on my suit—just had to get away because I didn't want to face Pops when he found out what I'd said."

I moved back through the narrow opening, the memories becoming clearer. "But I didn't realize that you'd followed me until we were all the way up here. And when I did, I was so angry. Because I knew Pops was going to be furious with me. Over what I'd said and that you had come after me, putting not only myself at risk but you too. But more than that"—I was horrified as the memory of that day came flooding back—"I hated you. I'd wanted to be alone, and there you were. Your stupid little face, looking so sad, just walking behind me. I didn't want you around. So I…" Shame spread through me, and I couldn't face Lucas. "I pushed you."

"Finally," Lucas said. "You remember. Now, move on to the good bit."

But I was stuck on the fact I'd pushed my brother so hard that he'd tumbled down the path and landed in the middle of a pile of rocks, which had given way with a sickening squish. Lucas had been covered in slime, and I'd been such a horrible, mixed-up ball of anger and fear that I'd simply turned and started running. I'd glanced over my shoulder at some point and had seen Lucas screaming and slipping as he tried to get up, the slime dripping off of him.

Well, at least I know where my nightmare came from, I thought with a shiver. "I'm so sorry. I never should have pushed you, let alone run off and left you."

"As I said before, I don't blame you—much—anymore. We were stupid kids. Where did you go? What did you see after you ran?" He lowered the gun and stepped toward me. "Tell me, and all of this will be over. I'll let you go, and whoever of your friends is still alive, they'll be free to go too. All I need to know is what happened to you after you pushed me."

"Why do you care?" I asked.

"Because whatever happened gave Pops the breakthrough he was looking for. But you weren't strong enough, and so he wiped your memories. But I would've been—"

"He did what?" I asked. *No way. There's no way.*

"If only he'd stopped coddling you and realized I had what you lacked. Pops—"

I had a plan—a horrible one, but it'd already been tested. I ran at Lucas and shoved as hard as I could. I had no way to know which of the rocks and boulders littering the landscape around us had been corrupted, but I knew at least a handful had to be. He should never have lowered his guard.

Lucas fell backward and hit the ground. I kicked his pack out of my way and lunged for the gun. Lucas tried to get up, but I kicked him hard in the ribs and grabbed his hand. Then I stepped to one side and pulled. With the adrenaline rush, I was able to flip Lucas over, and shutting off any emotion, I stepped on the back of his head, grinding him into the dirt and slime, trying to hold him down long enough for the waste bogs to do their worst. I pushed the gun down out of his hand and snarled.

"You're insane. And you won't get away with any of this. I'll make sure you're brought—"

I hadn't expected what Lucas did next. But I should've, all things considered. He shoved and twisted his arm—I heard the snap as something broke—and worked himself free. He got to his feet and staggered, the slime already eating away at his suit and working into his flesh. It was my nightmare turned reality.

So I did the only thing I could. I fired—once then again. Lucas fell to his knees, but his eyes never left mine.

"You can't stop me," he struggled to say then toppled over.

I had two coherent thoughts before the horror of what I did kicked in. I picked up Lucas's pack and thought, *<Cain, if you can hear me, for the love of Saturn, you need to find a way to get out of there. I've killed Lucas. Cain, I've—>*

That was it. No rational thought was left. I turned and ran past the boulders and straight through the walls with the glyphs.

11

Buried Memories

I might not have been so reckless if I hadn't been so horrified and ashamed of what had just taken place. Because then I might not have run pell-mell into something that should've been solid and knocked me out.

A few meters into the darkness, I stopped. I wanted to cry, but the tears didn't come. Instead, I felt dizzy, and my chest was tight. My skin tingled, and I was cold and shivering. I wasn't sure how long I stood there, shaking like an antique ship on its last thruster.

"What have I done?" I whispered into the darkness. Stopping Lucas had certainly been at the top of my to-do list, but killing him hadn't been the idea. We were going to bring him to justice, to show the known worlds that I was nothing like him, to clear my name, along with the added bonus of stopping an intergalactic war. But killing him hadn't been on the table, at least not on mine. The others might not have blinked an eye, but Lucas wasn't their brother. Nor did I have the training they surely would've gone through for that type of situation.

I desperately wished Cain was with me, not just

mentally but physically. I could've curled up in his arms and stayed that way for eternity.

After the worst of the shock passed, I took a few deep breaths and flipped on my suit's lights. Cain's not here. No one is here but me. There'll be time enough to deal with what you did. But for now, you've got to keep going. I said that a few times and forced myself to bury my emotions.

I dug through Lucas's pack. He'd come fairly well supplied. Rations, nutrient packs, rope, a palm pad, some miniature antigrav bots, and—thank goodness—two extra battery packs. I checked my suit's readout and noted its power was down to fifty-three percent. I considered switching them out but decided against it, not knowing how long I would be out there, and changing out the power packs too early might mean I wouldn't have enough juice to make it back. If that's even an option now.

First things first. I needed to figure out where I was. I slowly rotated in a full circle and had a flash of déjà vu. While the walls were constructed out of rock, I couldn't help but note the eerie feeling of being in the cavern on Dar. When I turned the way I was sure I'd come, I did a double take. All I saw was solid rock. When I turned in the opposite direction, the tunnel I was in seemed to extend for quite a ways, and I knew I hadn't run very far into the darkness.

Carefully, I made my way back toward the wall and gingerly reached out to touch it. Solid. My fear levels spiked again. But if this is solid, how in the worlds did I get in here? I couldn't come up with any plausible answer. Not an auspicious start to surviving this little misadventure.

The more important question, I realized, was not about how I'd gotten in but how many times I'd been there. As I stared at the wall and tilted my head to look up, the lights caught the edge of another geometrical pattern. It was rectangular with hundreds of smaller circles overlapping inside it. And where some of the circles created overlapping shapes—like curved triangles of a sort—the stone had been carved out, creating a deeply recessed area.

"Thirty-four," the number shot out of my mouth as I remembered.

When I ran away from the outpost then ran after shoving Lucas, through some impossible means, I'd ended up here. And I sat here, counting those spaces until I fell asleep. The memory was short on details, but I knew it was a memory.

A sharp pain pierced the back of my skull, and I bent over in agony, abruptly feeling nauseated. For a moment, I feared that meant something had happened to Cain, but as the pain receded, I sensed his presence, faint but there. Gulping air in, I straightened and ran a quick bioscan. The suit's readouts weren't as thorough as something Dr. Kell could do on the Samaritan, but at least they were something. My blood pressure was elevated, and the suit detected heightened activity in my hippocampus. Nothing critical. Yet.

Was Lucas right? Could Pops have suppressed my memories? As far as I was aware, no tech out there could completely wipe someone's memory. Plenty of drugs and underground quacks could temporarily send someone to la-la land to forget all their troubles or maybe bury trauma or unwanted events for a good long while. But I didn't think anything could extract memories and destroy them. On the other hand, the whisper nets did have a valid point—militaries and governments were always developing tech the public didn't know about. But would Pops have had access to that? Silly question. Even if he had, I wouldn't be remembering things. Duh. There'd be no recall at all.

I needed to get back on track. I was stuck inside a mountain in the red zone. Did that qualify as underground? If it did, I was probably going to die. No one went underground, even though xenologists drooled at the chance to explore the ruins they knew were hidden in the depths of Epo-5. But the centuries of toxic waste being dumped and leaching deep into the dirt had made any subterranean exploration impossible.

How the hell did I survive as a kid?

My insane brother had wanted me to remember and to bring him here. And whatever it was had been important enough that Pops made sure I didn't remember. Or was it really like what Lucas said, that I simply wasn't strong enough or enough of what Pops was hoping for? But as I stood there and chewed on that question, the sting of the insult was already fading. I didn't care if I was good enough or not. I was here. Now. Lucas might've been out of the picture, but his insane followers weren't. And I'd made a promise to the Third and meant to keep it.

I checked my suit. I'd been in the red zone for almost

four hours. That meant—if being underground didn't horribly speed up the process, and whom was I kidding?—I had roughly twenty hours before my suit would no longer be able to keep up with preventing radiation sickness. At least I've got a deadline, I tried to joke with myself. Deadlines were my jam. Before I realized my whole vacation voucher had been a setup, I'd really believed I'd earned that sucker. I was quick and efficient as a help desk aficionado and always met the call quotas upper management wanted to see.

I slung the pack over my shoulder and decided the time had come to take a trip down memory lane. Pun intended.

The trip was a bit longer than expected. Nobody would've guessed a little kid could've gotten so far. But as I made my way through the tunnel, taking note of how the ground slanted at a downward angle, the markings along the walls grew more and more familiar. I was certain I'd been in that tunnel before.

<Cain? I don't know if you can hear me, but if there's a chance you can, I'm heading down through a long tunnel of sorts. I'm seeing a whole bunch of markings that feel familiar. They're connected to the Third, if not made by the Third somehow.>

My suit continued to adjust for the changes in temperature, and the deeper I went, the warmer it became. I would need to change battery packs sooner than I'd hoped, at that rate. I stopped every fifteen minutes to try to regulate my body temperature and took advantage of the breaks to note the different carvings in the wall. The glyphs became increasingly refined the deeper I went, smaller and more intricate. Either the artists had refined their techniques, or the tools they'd used had improved. Or they'd been carved by the Third.

While I sensed a familiarity with the glyphs, I didn't have a clue what they meant. And that was beyond frustrating. Sam had worked through multiple translation programs and tried to extrapolate potential context, but without some kind of starting point, I had no way to figure it out. Maybe each glyph represented a single idea, word, or character in a potential written language or a potential mathematical basis for communication. One of the great conundrums about xenology was whether any conclusions were correct. That was one reason I figured time-travel tech would be awesome, minus the whole potential of destroying the timeline or somehow wiping oneself out of existence. Although that idea holds certain merits at the moment.

Hundreds upon hundreds of papers, classes, and debates had been dedicated to the question of whether a xenologist could be unbiased or would always view a different culture through the biased lens of the culture they grew up in. If that topic was of interest, I would highly recommend checking out that wormhole.

I leaned toward the belief that no matter how hard a xenologist might try, they would always carry some bias toward their own culture. When I considered the Third, I thought about them from my frame of reference, being a human—they had basic wants and needs, and they had felt the injustice of what had happened on Dar and longed to be free. But I had no way of really knowing if those human emotions and cultural constructs could be placed on the Third. If I was a Neetho xenologist, part of a collective hive mind, I might come to a totally different conclusion or at least extrapolate from a different starting point.

"I wonder what side of the equation you landed on, Pops," I mused.

I vaguely remembered a few of his lectures, but I was a teenager and not really too concerned with the ethics of bias. A xenologist had to take a lot on faith, which was one of the reasons the field demanded a meticulous nature from its practitioners. But it was also a continually evolving field, with new ideas, new discoveries, and information that updated as tech advanced.

Whoops. I said I wouldn't wander down that wormhole, but I did a bit.

I stopped once more and checked the suit. Not good. I was down to seventeen percent. Time to switch out a battery. I set the pack down and squatted to dig through it for what I needed. At least that tech is interchangeable. The ruling that all basic life support equipment should be compatible had come about during the Umio Scramble, a brief dustup with the Glipglows in the early stages of their relationship with the known worlds.

After hooking up the new battery, I slipped the old into the pack, and my fingers brushed against the palm pad. Curious, I pulled it out. What kind of things would Lucas have stored in here? Are there pics of his family?

I shoved it back into the pack. I killed my own brother. The words ran loud and clear in my head. But he would've killed me. But can the justification of self-defense erase the guilt? I knew the answer to that as I leaned my head against the wall and cried.

I pulled out the palm pad again and took a deep breath. Feeling sorry for myself wasn't going to help. The pad lit up, and a holo menu sprang to life. For a split second, I perked up when I saw the option to send messages. But as I clicked through, I found I was too far underground. Besides, who would I send a message to? I didn't know what had happened with Cain and the others and had no way to know if Miles or Lio were in the system or not.

I touched the icon for personal documents, and when the list appeared, my fingers tightened around the sleek edges of the palm pad. Hundreds of documents were there, all labeled and time-stamped. And all were by the same author, Wats Hawking Orion. Lucas had brought along Pops's journals.

12

Who Was
Wats Hawking Orion?

As I skimmed the list of documents, I realized they weren't duplicates of the journals I'd read. It was a good thing I was sitting down. I picked one at random, time-stamped 2573.5.19. *This would've been before I was born.* I did the math. *Pops would've been only about fifteen years old at the time.*

The document opened, and I chose to listen to the embedded recording, which turned out to be along the lines of a personal journal entry:

"Mat says that the guard rotations are too tight, that there's no way we could make it past security. But Cam and I are in agreement. We've got twenty-three seconds to make it around the outer wall. Mat's just too slow. But I know we can make it. Once we get past security, it'll be easy to hack into the biolocks. Mr. Harpoth and the director gave us all the tools we'll need. No sweat. We'll nab the goods and make a clean break for it."

I hit Pause and stared at the screen. *What in the worlds am I listening to?* At fifteen, Pops would've still been working alongside his family and looking forward to getting into a schooling branch.

"The director says a ship will be waiting for us on the western launch pad. And if we make it, then we've got a sure way in. Mom isn't thrilled about this admissions test. Says in her time things were a lot more cerebral—whatever that's about. Dad's optimistically cautious. I've passed all the genetic tests, everything they could throw at us. I even heard one of the docs say they never thought they'd see the culmination of the work in their lifetime. I'm hot stuff."

"Dear God, he's talking about the Sun Worshipers," I said.

I sat up a little straighter and took a closer look at the entries, playing snippets from several different documents. The whole thing was an autobiography of sorts—what his life had truly been about. Lucas had been holding all the answers. *And for how long? How long had he had access to these and known the truth?* A fresh wave of guilt rolled over me as I realized that was something I'd probably never find out.

I wanted to sit there and start at the beginning and work my way through them all, to finally be able to understand who Pops had been and see if I could come to terms with what he'd done. But I didn't have the time, not stuck down in an underground tunnel on one of the most radioactive planets in the known worlds. Really, I was interested in only two time frames, the entries from our time on Epo-5 and the last one.

With a shaking hand, I brought up the last entry, time-stamped 2605.6.24, a year before the Cricade Wars ended and Pops was arrested:

"Magistrate Ru-ut One—I'm not even sure 'magistrate' is the right word—has finally sent a reply. I will give the Eeri credit where credit is due. Their level of spycraft and security coding is some of the best I've ever seen. I was given three sets of coordinates and a basic crumbling matrix to work out which of the three will be the meeting site. While Mrs. Gol and I have further distanced ourselves from each other—I will never regret my marriage—I can't fault the woman and all the work she's done to help prepare me. If the meeting brings about results, we may finally have the answers we've been searching for. My only wish is that it hadn't come at the expense of my children. But I've done what I can to ensure their protection. If the Eeri don't have what we're looking for or they decide to betray me, then I'll go ahead with what I'll have to do to make sure Mahia and Lucas are taken care of. If only Mahia had… None of that matters anymore. All I want is for the two of them to be safe. And maybe in the future, they'll find a way to finish what I've started. What we've started. May the rays of abundance embrace them both."

I shut off the palm pad and, with a sense of detachment, carefully tucked it back into the pack. Then I stood, took a deep breath, and shouldered the pack. My pops, my father, no—a man named Wats Hawking Orion had been sent on a mission by Mrs. Gol and the Sun Worshipers to meet with the Eeri. He hadn't gone over to humanity's enemy with a hope of ending the war or some noble reason why he believed he should help the Eeri. He'd gone to them because he'd belonged to and worked for a group of purists who'd been pursuing some kind of technology or knowledge that required a specific genetic makeup in order to access the smart bots, in order to communicate with the Third.

Wats wasn't the hero of this story. Nor was he the misunderstood and downtrodden figure in my life. He'd been one of the bad guys.

So why am I wasting my time, scurrying around in the dark after something the damned purists were after? I didn't want anything to do with it, not with them or Wats. *Forget this. Just shove it all out an airlock. I'm done.*

I spun around and headed back to where I'd entered the tunnels. Even though the wall was solid, if Cain and the others managed to get free, they could bring up the GPS data from my suit to see where I'd gone. That was a logical decision. If I was going to get rescued, that would be the place to go and wait. And maybe I could figure out how I'd gotten through the wall in the first place. Perhaps I'd hit a hidden control panel and, in my panic, not realized what I'd done. I could try several different options.

I wasn't nearly as detached from my seething emotions as I'd thought I was. Halfway back to where I'd entered the tunnels, I stopped, threw the pack against the wall, and screamed. "What were you? How could you have been one of *them* when you were with us? I know you weren't perfect, but give me a break. A full-on Sun Worshiper up until the end? How can I trust that you even really cared about me? Or was I just some kind of a means to an end for you? That ended up as a huge disappointment to you."

The whole scene was a bit childish, but I'd nurtured this heroic image of Pops for years. I'd seared it into my brain, using it as a shield against all the people who'd hated him and, in turn, hated me. But I had nothing left to hide behind, no elusive discovery to vindicate him. The truth was out, and it wasn't what I'd been hoping for.

I punched the wall—stupid, since I was sure I'd already broken my pinky finger—and further scuffed up my already compromised suit. I pulled back and shook my hand at the rush of pain. "Son of a—" I stopped and stared.

In my anger, I wasn't aiming for anything in particular, but I'd punched one of the glyphs. The carved lines were softly glowing a pale blue.

"Scuttling scuttle crabs," I said, reaching out to touch an adjacent glyph, which glowed, too, as my hand lifted off its uneven surface.

But how? Mesmerized, I shuffled a few steps to my

right, raised my hands, and touched two more glyphs. The right glyph glowed, while the left didn't. I looked at my injured hand—*Who would've thought compromising the integrity of my suit would actually be helpful?*—and gently pressed it against another glyph. As I slowly moved back and stared at the light, I remembered the Third in the cavern on Dar and what the Darquets had done to them.

In a fit of temporary insanity—which I thought could be forgiven—I ran up and down the tunnel, touching as many of the glyphs as I could reach. For a few moments, the entire tunnel was bathed in a soft blue light. Each glyph faded in time, and after my giddiness diminished, I timed a few. Each one glowed for two minutes and fifteen seconds. No matter where I moved in the tunnel, the timing was the same.

So many questions were piling up on top of other questions that I didn't know where to start. Well, that wasn't entirely true. I did have somewhere to start but didn't want to. I found I had a decision to make. If I'd been there before—and I was sure that I had—then something had to be in Wats's journal entries, perhaps even the reason why he'd suppressed my memories of what had happened. And, of course, the pesky little guilt trip about what I'd promised to the Third. *But I don't want anything to do with what he was up to. Or Lucas. They can rot, for all I care.* But *maybe there's still a glimmer of hope,* I argued with myself. *Maybe this is all about trying to help the Third and the Star Eaters, however they're connected.*

"Who am I kidding?" I sighed. *When did governments and secret organizations work for the benefit of others and not themselves? Not very often, unfortunately.*

No, Miles was probably right. The Sun Worshipers and Yilmaz and whoever else were after power—or at least what they perceived as power.

But I'm not. I don't care about any of that crap. My promise was to help the Third. It had nothing to do with Wats or Lucas or anyone else. I do that, and then I'm done, finished with this whole mess. Cain and I can leave and go make a life for ourselves far away from all this.

My decision meant two things—well, three. I needed to go back and get the pack, I would need to go farther into the tunnels, and I would need to keep listening to the journal entries.

13

Anything but a Normal Life

Time stamp 2596.3.7:

"The air conditioning units are down again. We've petitioned for an upgrade but so far have been denied. I swear if they want me to keep working on this project, they're going to have to prioritize some funding. The board of directors, though, the lazy slops, continue to tell me their backers are on the fence—some political junk about a dustup on Mandarian's Rhine. Everyone's getting nervous about the longevity of our work. No one said this would be easy. Ugh. I really need a break.

"Mahia and Lucas show aptitude. Their genetic profiles are in line with what we've been working toward. I'm still not keen on sending them off to training. Not yet. I'd like to try to up their skills some before that time comes. But who am I kidding? I'm just being a tad bit selfish. I just don't want to send them into that situation yet.

Neither one of them knows what's going on, and they won't be well received either. Mrs. Gol will see to that. She's too shortsighted. We needed a fresh round of genetics in the gene pool. But Mahia and Lucas are going to have to toughen up if they want to make it through this."

After a pause, Wats could be heard drinking something. He coughed a couple of times then started in again.

"I swear if they don't get these units fixed, we're all going to go crazy. I'm running out of ideas for what to do with the kids, and it's too hot to do much work outside. We've got about two more weeks of this foul weather if Bullin is correct, and she usually is. God, she'd better be."

I stopped the playback. Skimming through the rest of it, I moved on to the next entry. I couldn't remember exactly when I'd run off and everything had gone sideways, but I knew it'd been toward the first months of our time on Epo-5.

Time stamp 2596.3.12:

"Mahia continues to show promise. She's picking up on concepts faster than I did, and I think Lucas will show a greater aptitude than hers. I think I'm going to switch over to some—"

The recording abruptly cut off. I checked the

document and realized that was it. The next entry was time-stamped a week later. My finger hovered over the menu. *Just do it. Listen to it and remember. Get it over with. The sooner the better.*

Time stamp 2596.3.19:

"I'm not even sure… No. This is exactly what we were looking for. Hoping for. But if only it hadn't happened like this. Everything is in jeopardy. I don't want to have to make a choice, but it's not looking good. Lucas is still in the medical suite. Dr. Lumen says it'll probably be another week or two before Lucas is conscious. It's a miracle Opal and Sert were doing up-and-down scouting that day, or else neither one of my kids might have been found. Given Opal's location when she found Lucas and Sert's location within the tunnels, we had the right place to start looking for Mahia.

"Silvia apologized for disagreeing with me. I don't blame her, even though we lost a whole day, looking for Mahia. Neither one of us has an explanation as to how Mahia got into the tunnels. We can't find an opening anywhere near where we found Lucas. And Mahia is still refusing to talk. I've taken her back three times now, and she won't open up. I wish she was older and could understand the importance of what happened, of what she stumbled across. When Lucas wakes up, I'll have to see if he saw anything that would be useful. I doubt it, but I have to try.

"Mahia, though… I just don't know. I've got the rover checked out for tomorrow afternoon, and we're going to head back up there one more time. If she doesn't talk, then I'll visit with Dr. Lumen about my options. I can't have her holding on to information she won't share. There's too a high chance it could end up in the wrong hands."

Lucas had been right. Wats had blocked my memories after all. *So I must not have talked.* I felt a flare of pride at that. *I did something brave, something to thwart the Sun Worshipers, even though I had no idea what I was doing at the time.*

The tunnel had widened by the time that entry wrapped up. I walked for a few more minutes in silence and discovered the tunnel opened up into a decent-sized space, presenting me with four options. The tunnel continued in front of me, with two other tunnel openings, one to my left and one to my right. The walls were covered in glyphs at that point, and I had no idea which direction to go.

"What would I have done as a kid?" I mused. I would have been frightened and tired. And I would've had little-kid logic—*meaning none.* Going with my gut, I turned to my right.

In roughly five or six meters, the tunnel stopped. I cranked up the lights on my suit to the brightest setting—pretty impressed with their output—and saw I'd arrived at the edge of a ledge, some sort of cavern, from what I could see. But I didn't have enough expertise to know whether it was natural or artificial. My best guess was artificial, given my traipsing around in the tunnels.

This is what I was afraid of as a kid? I carefully moved as close to the edge as I dared and flashed my wrist light around, eating through my suit's power to try to illuminate the darkness, but I could hardly see anything roughly a meter or so in front of me.

I took a step back and rummaged through the pack. All the items Lucas had stuffed in there felt essential. "You certainly came prepared," I said then clammed up. *Neither one of us had truly come prepared. Time for a break.*

After moving away from the edge, I sat down and checked my suit. I'd lost four hours, and my suit's power was down to sixty-three percent. *I might finally figure some things out, but I'm not sure I'm going to live long enough to tell anyone.* Honestly, I wasn't sure I cared at that point.

Time to listen to the next entry.

Time stamp 2596.3.23:

"Mahia actually put up a fuss this time. Doesn't want to go with me. Ended up in hysterics. I hated myself, but I gave her a sedative and loaded her up in the rover. Am I doing the right thing? Is this worth what it's doing to her? I'm not even sure I care if she talks or not at this point. Whatever happened was horrible enough that it might be better to block her memories anyway. Let her lead a different life, one that isn't wrapped up in all of this. If Lucas pulls through, I might turn my focus toward him. Let Mahia just be.

"We're almost to the site. Mahia's calmed down and doesn't seem as frightened this time. Maybe she'll pull through. God, I hope so. I don't know what I'll do if I lose one of them too… That's not helping. Get your head on straight.

"We're back, and I've made my decision. I'm going to have Dr. Lumen do a memory block. He said he could do a temporary one for now then, when we're back at Cloud-7, have one of the docs there do a permanent block. At least this way, Mahia can have a normal life. Lucas can carry on for me. I'll work on getting these notes in order after I check in on Lucas."

I had to stop listening and wipe away the tears. *I don't know how much more of this I can take. I hate you… and I don't. You loved me… I think. Right? But can I love you, knowing what I do now?*

A wave of exhaustion washed over me, and I leaned against a wall, letting my head fall back. "A normal life. It's been anything but that."

I closed my eyes and tried to picture what a normal life might've looked like—married, maybe a xenologist or a profession parallel to that field somehow, perhaps a couple of kids, family dinners on the days off, a brother with his wife and his two children coming over for holidays, a father who doted on his grandchildren. Or maybe I would've chosen a different field, thrown myself into my career, and made a name for myself, being whisked off to give lectures or rub shoulders with government officials. Perhaps I would just live a quiet life, working a job I enjoyed, embracing solitude, and taking a few vacations here and there to remind myself of the adventures I'd had as a kid. The possibilities were endless when considering a normal life. *If you can even define what the word* "normal" *really stands for.*

I rolled my head to the left and stared out into the cavern. Closing my eyes, I forced myself to return to the horrible nightmare of when I'd shoved Lucas down and run. I shivered and wanted to avoid that pain, but I needed to know what had happened to me.

<Cain, I wish you were here. I could sure use your help right about now.>

Lucas's devastated face popped up over and over again. I shouted at him, pushed him, turned, and ran— like my brain was stuck on a perpetual loop. I leaned forward and squeezed my eyes shut until they hurt, trying to stay with the memory.

I shouted, pushed, turned, and ran, heading toward the boulders. I ran at the rock wall, blinded by tears and shame and fear.

I shouted, pushed, turned, and ran, crying wildly, so afraid of what I'd done, not brave enough to turn around and go for help, having to face Pops.

I shouted, pushed, turned, and ran, afraid I'd killed him. I thought I had. I looked around, my eyes wide, my breath coming in painful gasps. I had nowhere to go. The boulders loomed above me, and I felt them judging me, staring at me, moving to crush me. The ground trembled, and the boulders shifted.

Pain ripped through my head, and I screamed into the darkness, into the past, and into the present. Then the darkness swallowed me whole.

14

A Web of Secrets

Light shimmered and shifted like water, gently lapping at my feet. I was sitting on the edge of a beach, and I leaned backward to sink my fingers into the warm black sand. Twisting strands of blue lights danced through the air above me, turning into a myriad of shapes for an instant before forming a new one.

To my left, the sand shifted, but I felt no fear. The grains of sand vibrated and danced until up out of the ground, a thin black strand of something soft and malleable appeared. It pushed through the sand, the fine black grains of sand raining off it as it tilted back then fell forward. It lay there for a moment, then it, too, changed shape to form a bloated triangle. The blue lights moved together as one then converged on the strange figure.

The scene wasn't displaying a predator-and-prey relationship. I wasn't sure how I knew that, but I did. The triangular creature—for lack of a better word—let the dancing blue lights wrap around its sleek, black flesh, forming smaller replicas of the shapes I'd seen in the sky. Another strand then a third burst through the sand, all matching the shape of the first. When all three looked alike, they turned and moved together to form a type of three-petaled flower. The blue lights moved up into the sky, made the same shape again, then darted off over the sea of light.

The strange creatures remained, gently twisting back and forth in unison. I had no idea how long the lights were gone, for I felt no sense of time in that place. But when they returned, they weren't alone.

The light off in the distance had formed two human-oid shapes. Their heads were wide and flat, but each had two arms and two legs. Each light being had an arm raised at chest level, with a hand extended, palm side up. The blue lights swirled above the hands, creating an orblike appearance, and where their feet touched the light, which moved liked water, the area glowed.

I stood, dusting off the sand, knowing I needed to ask some questions. The light beings turned toward me, their eyeless faces somehow looking straight through me.

"Who are you? What are you?" I asked.

In unison, both light beings tilted their heads to the side. The dancing blue lights shifted into two different shapes. One became a pulsating square, with another square rotated at forty-five degrees. The other shape was a circle with a herringbone pattern inside.

"I'm sorry, I don't understand what those mean. Are they specific words or a concept?"

Future. Instruction. Need.

Those three words rang loud and clear in my head, along with something else—the Third. "How is this possible? I was"—the words were difficult to find in that place—"somewhere. I don't think—no, I didn't think I still—"

The shapes shifted, and hundreds of tiny triangles were flowing up and down one of the light being's arms, while the other stretched and grew into a spiral.

Need. Promise. Future.

I shook my head. "I still don't understand."

The light beings turned toward one another, and the shapes moved together then burst apart into three separate orbs. Thin tendrils of the blue light unwound from each orb and joined with another to create one interconnected shape. Their pulsating light grew until it was too bright to look at. As I raised a hand to shield my eyes, the light exploded. When I dared to look again, the blue lights and the strange beings were gone.

Pain spread across the back of my head, and the landscape dimmed. "No, wait! I still need help, some way to translate what you're trying to—" I blinked and was back in the tunnels.

"How is any of this possible?" I groaned and rubbed my temples. I had no doubt of what I'd seen. *But the Third replaced the smart bots, and they'd left my body, back on Dar. Was there some kind of residual aftereffects? Imprints, maybe?* An even better question poked at me once the pain dissipated. *I was trying to remember what had happened to me on Epo-5, and that was what I recalled? Or saw? Could the two issues be related?*

"This isn't helping," I muttered. Staying where I was and endlessly speculating wasn't going to give me answers. I couldn't go forward, so I needed to go back and pick a different tunnel. *Or just listen to the next recording.*

"Fine," I grumbled. *I'll do both.*
Time stamp 2596.3.29:

"I'm not sure how to explain any of this. And I'm not sure I'm going to try. If the others knew… no. I almost lost her. I won't lose her again. There'd be nothing left of her after they got done researching what happened. There's got to be another way to come at all of this. Lucas can help. I'll work with him, take what I need from Mahia, and incorporate it with Lucas.

"What I can report back to the others will be what they wanted to hear anyways, what we suspected was here. That makes three planets that we know of. Epo-5, Selarious, and the Telt home world. I know there's rampant speculation about Dar as well but no confirmed information as of yet.

"What I've seen so far on Epo-5 matches up with the maps and information we've gathered on the Telt home world. I suspect after this assignment, I'll be sent to Selarious to corroborate what the teams have been working on over there.

"With the underground network of tunnels, I'm hoping they'll lead us to fabrication chambers. I have to wonder if the reason this world was decimated has something to do with the alpha fragments. That would be a theory to pass on to Dr. Aydem. Let him see if he finds any connections.

He may need to dig into the mythology of the Sici for clues.

"As for Epo-5, initial survey and scans are showing at least three potential fabrication chambers, with a possibility of two more. The tunnels are collapsed along the route to one potential chamber, and radioactive levels are too high—even for the equipment I've been supplied with—to get to the other. Dr. Lumen is still unsure how Mahia survived. She should have been dead from radiation poisoning by the time I found her. Four days she was down here. The suit kept her hydrated, but... the rest? I trust Dr. Lumen but erred on the side of caution and paid him an exorbitant number of credits as well. I don't believe he'll take his results to anyone else. He's a father, too, and I believe he understands."

"Four days?" I said. "There's no way I heard that correctly." I scrolled back and listened to that section twice. He'd said four days, loud and clear. *That's impossible.* But most of what had happened to me recently should've been impossible. *So... yeah.* I stopped for a moment and clicked off the suit's lights. *Nope, not glowing.* I had to check.

When I turned the lights back on, the ground trembled, not a little shiver but a full-on quake. I reached out to steady myself against the wall and took a look at my suit's readout. Data was minimal and unhelpful. I was too far underground and out of reach of any kind of uplink. None of the research on Epo-5 had discussed earthquakes. A soft blue light caught my attention, and I realized I'd touched one of the glyphs. As the light spread through the carved lines of the symbol, I grinned and did a little dance. "Hot dog."

I was staring at a depiction of three orbs with lines drawn to connect them. *Is that coincidence or the universe helping out? Nope. Not even going to question this.*

I touched the glyph again and used the palm pad to snap a few pics. Being so relieved at finally finding something I might be able to figure out, I momentarily forgot about the quakes.

The sound of a muffled thud preceded the next earthquake, and its tremor was much stronger and longer. *At least over thirty seconds. Pops alluded to other entrances to these tunnels. So there's definitely got to be another way out.* I checked the suit. I had a few more hours before I needed to switch over to the last power pack, and I was still fighting against the deadline when the radiation would overwhelm the suit's capabilities. *Pick up the pace.*

I moved through the tunnel, quickly scanning the glyphs, but didn't see anything else that lined up with what I'd been shown. Before I knew it, I was back at the chamber where I'd decided to go right. Not hesitating, I just kept on walking and plunged into another tunnel.

Soon, I stopped dead in my tracks. "Holy Jupiters," I whispered.

The tunnel was no longer made out of rock but bone. I lifted a wrist and examined the wall to my right, slowly moving the light across the ceiling then down along the wall to my left. It was one hundred percent bone, thousands of pieces of bone. Some were fairly easy to identify—skulls, scapulae, ribs, femurs, and more. Not only that, but the way the bones had been arranged hadn't been at random. They'd been laid down in specific patterns that I recognized not only from my most recent vision but from the previous images I'd captured on Dar and their matches on Epo-5.

The geometric patterns were the same. They were a little rough, considering the chosen material but definitely not a coincidence. *But who'd done the patterns first? The inhabitants of Epo-5 or the Third? Or better yet, am I looking at the Third somehow?* No, I didn't think so. I dismissed that idea fairly quickly. I was confident in believing the blue lights and the strange creature from the sand were somehow a part of the Third. How they'd made the transition from what I saw there versus the fungal structure on Dar, I didn't know. And as I affirmed that theory, I realized I had another connection I was pretty sure would hold up.

On Lunar 5, when I met up with the Star Eaters, they'd lifted their hoods, and the light from underneath had temporarily blinded me. *They're the light beings. So I was right. The Third and the Star Eaters are connected.* Exactly how, I wasn't sure. But at least some things were clicking into place. *I hope Miles was able to find those slippery eels. And they'd better be a bit more forthcoming this time.*

So engrossed in congratulating myself, I didn't really pay attention to the second muffled thud of the day. The following quake was the worst one yet. The floor rippled from the aftershocks, and I stumbled. Involuntary reactions were supposed to be nature's way of protecting oneself, but they didn't work that way that time.

My hands shot out in front of me, and I sidestepped to the left, tripped over my own stupid feet, and fell right into the bone wall. A sculptured piece of rib pierced my hand, and—believe me—I screamed a few salty phrases. Making it back to the surface didn't matter anymore. The bone not only did a number on my hand but, as luck would have it, easily ripped the part of the suit that'd been damaged. I didn't have a patch kit, so I was fully exposed to the radiation.

I slumped down to the floor and stared at my exposed skin. *With the radiation levels underground, my skin should start to bubble and boil in three… two… one…*

Nothing. My creamy skin didn't turn a nasty red, split open, and ooze with pus—minus the nice stab wound, of course. I flipped my hand back and forth. Nothing. I checked my vitals. Everything was within accepted parameters. *Were the radiation stories a lie just to keep people out?* I didn't think so, since the journal entries had made a comment about not being able to go in some of the tunnels because of the risk of exposure. *So why wasn't I melting into a puddle of goo?*

Light reflected off the bones, and I raised my hand to shield my eyes. The light bounced up and down, and I heard voices. I tried to get to my feet, but a wave of dizziness overtook me, forcing me to stay down. The floor shifted back and forth as it shuddered again. Something was beneath the surface, trying to get out. The ground pushed up underneath my hands then my feet. I scrambled back, but whatever it was, was following me.

The ground broke beneath me just as a person stepped forward, the light from their suit illuminating me. I looked up at my rescuer and tried to reach out to grab their hand.

But the earth swallowed me whole as I shouted, "Cain!"

15

Is It Now, or Was It Then?

I was terrified. I'd killed my brother. *What is Pops going to do to me?* No, that was ages before. I was terrified. My skin should be bubbling and boiling, my insides cooking hotter than a Neetho's food-stall kitchen. *What will Cain think of me? I've killed my own brother.*

I'd been running away, and something even worse had found me. I should be dead. I was dead.

<Mahia, it's me. I'm here. But you need to try and relax. Don't fight against what's happening.>

Who said that?

Pops? I'm so sorry, Pops. I didn't mean to. It was an accident. I sobbed and turned away from his face. But he gently wrapped his arms around me and pulled me close. I struggled for a moment then buried my face against his chest. *I'm sorry, Pops. I didn't mean to.* Over and over again, the words echoed through my head.

The ground rumbled, and the rock walls were so tall, and I was so small. I was trapped and didn't know where to go. The tears obscured my vision, and I stumbled and fell, cutting my suit on the ground.

I sat down and wailed, tucking my injured hand close to my body.

Something swam through the dirt and slime, a long, sinuous piece of black fiber. I hiccupped and wiped away my tears, smearing blood across my cheeks. Two more strands pushed through the ground and joined the first. Fear forced me to freeze. They changed shape, and something horrible and foul and smelly pushed up out of the ground. Three mouths opened where the strands of black fiber had been, and three dark pits moved toward me. I screamed, and the darkness swallowed me whole.

I was back in Pops's arms, being gently rocked back and forth. My hands gripped the stretchy material of his suit, and I clung to him. *Don't hate me, Pops. Please. I didn't mean to.*

<Mahia, relax. Surrender to the memories. Your mind is trying to tell you something.>

I killed him. Oh, Jupiter. I killed my own brother. Shot him. No, I pushed him. Forgive me.

Warmth spread through my mind as a ray of light pushed back the darkness. The image of Pops melted away into the memory of two children laughing and running through a meadow. *I know this… but how?*

A man stepped into the light, and I held up a hand to try to make out who it was.

"Pops?"

The man shook his head and stepped toward me. I caught a flicker of movement behind his legs.

"Cain," I said and ran to him. I threw my arms around him and held him tightly. "What's happening? How are you here? Where… where are we?"

"We're in my memory. Remember the one I shared? With my father and sister?"

"Yes. I think so. But weren't we on Epo-5? I was… somewhere else. Right?"

Cain brushed back my hair and kissed my forehead. "Yes. And we still are. The details can wait. Right now, we need to sort out what's happening in your mind."

I pulled away, heat rising to my cheeks. "No. I don't think I want to remember. I did… something horrible." I turned away. "You'll hate me," I whispered.

He grabbed my hand and pulled me back to him. "I could never hate you." He turned me around and leaned forward and placed a gentle kiss against my lips. "Show me. I'm here, right here with you."

I wanted to resist, but when I looked up into his amber eyes, filled with compassion and love, I surrendered. He touched his forehead to mine, and together we remembered.

I looked back at Lucas, covered in slime, his skin already red and bleeding. His tears and screams filled me with fear. I didn't know what to do or where to go, so I turned and ran. I knew Pops would hate me and that I would be taken away. I'd done something so horrible, so unforgivable. But Lucas was my brother. I was his big sister. I was supposed to look after him. I stopped running and tried to catch my breath. I was a big girl. Pops had even let me watch Lucas once all by myself. Ms. Bettle hadn't even had to come and check on us. Pops trusted me, and Lucas needed me.

When I turned to go back to my brother, I tripped and fell. I cut my hands on something sharp, and my forehead felt like it was on fire. I struggled to sit up. My suit had been damaged. I heard Pops's voice lecturing Lucas and me on how important it was to keep our suits in working order, to be careful and not damage them, or we'd have to spend a long time in medical. I didn't want that. I hated the decontamination protocols.

As I stood, something pushed through the ground in front of me. I took a step back, afraid, and stumbled against something else that had erupted out of the ground. Then a third piece of a nightmare pushed up out of the ground, and I watched in terror as they rose up together and circled me. As they moved, the ground shook, and I began to sink.

I screamed as the ground swallowed me whole.

<I'm still here. This is just a memory. Nothing here can hurt you.>

The strange voice comforted me, and I didn't feel quite so afraid. I awoke to a sea of twinkling blue lights dancing all around me. "Pops?" My voice echoed in the dark.

I cried a little, then when the tears ran out, I tried to stand up. A wave of dizziness overwhelmed me, and I had to stay sitting. In front of me, the darkness shifted, and I screamed. The blue lights faded, and the darkness slithered toward me, and I screamed and screamed and screamed. As it reared up, a giant slab of blackness came crashing down around me.

The darkness pierced my flesh and dug through my muscle and fat to my bone. I screamed until I was hoarse. All I knew was pain. It was overwhelming, and I couldn't think as I was ripped apart piece by piece.

<Mahia. You're not there. This is a memory. But you're safe. Don't get lost inside the memory. Come and stand beside me. Use me as your strength.> The voice called to me over and over until I turned my head and saw a man standing off to the side. His eyes looked kind, and he smiled as he extended a hand.

<That's it. I'm right here.>

I reached up and took his hand. Cain. This man was Cain. My heart's blood. I let him pull me up, and I looked back at the child I'd been, lying prone on a stone floor. I let him wrap an arm around my shoulder, and I leaned into his warmth and his strength. Now, I could look upon the memory with a sense of detachment.

Laid out on the floor, I had a huge gash across my forehead, and both of my palms were bloody. My exposed flesh was burned from radiation exposure, and I couldn't see my chest rising and falling.

<I died?>

What I'd thought had been shadow wasn't. It was a strange creature moving toward me. Its surface dull, it seemed to move in a liquid form, sliding across the ground. It reached out and touched me, and where it did, a soft blue glow appeared within its strange flesh. It spun a thin tendril of itself and reached out and ran itself across my forehead. The soft blue light intensified, and the creature changed shape into a geometric pattern.

<The Third.>

Another part of the Third moved out from the darkness and formed a different pattern. The two parts shifted back and forth as though in conversation over something.

<Me. They're debating about me. Oh my God.> I looked at Cain, who nodded in understanding.

<Keep watching.>

The two parts of the Third eventually changed into the same shape at the same time. They'd come to an understanding. Thin tendrils of the Third spun off each part, reared up, and pierced my body. My child's body didn't move or scream, and I knew one thing for certain. I had died on Epo-5, and the Third had brought me back to life.

I couldn't tell how much time passed as the Third worked to heal me, but they eventually pulled back, and my eyes fluttered open. As my child memory beheld my saviors, I opened my mouth and screamed. Then I got up and ran.

Cain and I moved quickly to follow as my child memory ran through the tunnels, crying and sobbing. I ran and ran and ran until I was exhausted. Then I sat down on the floor and slept. The cycle repeated itself over and over. I would run, wear myself out, then lie down and sleep. At some point, I stopped and collapsed, curling up into a tight ball on the floor. As I took a look around, I realized where we were. When I turned to Cain to tell him that, I saw a light bobbing in the distance.

Pops. He'd come after me to find me.

"Here! She's here!" he cried out. He ran to me with Ms. Bettle following behind. "Oh, my little Eima. What happened?"

"Is she alive?" Ms. Bettle asked, kneeling next to Pops.

"Yes. She's got a pulse. But how? Look at her suit. It's been torn," Pops said and pointed.

"Doesn't matter right now. Let's get her back to medical. This is a miracle. Two miracles this week, Wats."

Pops scooped me up, and I watched as I tried to get away but then snuggled up against his chest. "Shh, it's okay, love. Everything's going to be okay. I've got you now."

<Well, that certainly fills in a lot of the questions,> I said and turned toward Cain.

<Agreed. Are you ready to wake up?>

<Only if you're there waiting for me.>

<I am.>

16

The Cavalry Has Arrived

"Don't let her move," someone said.

"I know how to take care of her," Cain snapped.

"Went through some fancy first aid classes, did we? Radiation exposure training? Or how about how to deal with creepy, dark—"

At a growl from Cain, the voice stopped. *I know that voice.* "Miles?"

"In the flesh, my darling," he said.

I blinked and tried to get my bearings. I wasn't in the tunnels anymore. *A tent?*

"Reinforced smart-fabric. We've set up camp just outside the red zone," Cain said. "Courtesy of you-know-who."

"A little annoyed by that, are we?" I teased and winced. "Oh, man. Have I got the worst headache."

"Chambers will be by to check on you. Right now, he's helping stabilize Ochoa."

A realization hit me like a ton of debris. "Wait. Then… Aj-Otha." I closed my eyes and felt sick to my stomach.

"No. He's here too. I know what they wanted you to think, but Shelia didn't shoot any of us. All for show. I'm assuming they weren't ready to cut their losses."

I opened my eyes and stared at Cain. "Truth?"

He nodded. *<Truth.>*

"How did I get here? Wait, how did you find me?" I asked, struggling to sit up. My head ached, and everything was a jumble, as if the universe had decided to go into business for itself and create a million-piece jigsaw puzzle of my life.

"I wouldn't do that if—" Miles started but stopped when I glared at him.

Cain knew better than to argue and helped me sit up.

"Remember when we talked about how"—Cain threw a look at Miles—"being heart's blood meant a few changes? Like the telepathy, proximity, and heightened awareness of each other's emotions?"

"Yeah," I replied.

"I didn't know what happened, only that you were suddenly overwhelmed with fear, grief, shame… Let's just say a potent mixture of emotions. I didn't handle that well. Shelia got a call, and all hell broke loose. She was shouting orders, the men were scrambling, and it was exactly the opening we needed. We captured two of their men—one is in critical condition and, from what we've been told, has a low chance of surviving—and Chambers took a rather nasty shot to the leg. But we managed to get free. Probably wouldn't have if not for that call Shelia got. They had more important things to think of than us. Next thing I knew, Miles showed up." He glanced at Miles. "You never told me if it was just good timing or if you'd been waiting to see what happened."

"Good timing," Miles replied with a cheeky grin.

"And was it good timing that Lucas was able to use you against us? The data packet we picked up checked out. That it was sent by you." I really wasn't trying to accuse him, but the irritation radiating off of Cain was contagious, and my head was starting to ache again.

"I've already been absolved by Ochoa. I did send the data packet, but it would appear someone at Rockerton's has been sporting a little tattoo and bypassed security," Miles replied with a sniff of disdain.

"I was under the impression Rockerton's was secure," I said.

"It's safe to assume nothing is secure now," Cain replied.

Our circle of trust was getting smaller by the minute. And I wasn't used to the risk of taking leaps of faith in others. But I did know if I let myself get caught up in a guessing game of who was in whose pocket, I would drive myself insane.

<So, Lucas. What happened with him gave you the opportunity you needed?>

Cain nodded. *<Yes. The timing matches up.>*

"Care to fill me in?" Miles asked.

I didn't want to but did. "I shot Lucas. Killed him."

Miles looked at Cain then back at me. "Did you, now?"

"I just confessed to shooting my own brother, and that's all you have to say?" I snapped. I abruptly saw two of Miles and shook my head to clear my vision.

"First of all," Miles replied, the teasing tone gone, "you survived. And I'm assuming you were defending yourself?"

I nodded.

"Good. Then I absolve you of your guilt. Mahia, dear, we're at war. Whether you want to admit it or not. And with Lucas taken care of, we may be able to stop a whole lot more people from dying. As cliché as it sounds, you cut the head off the snake, and, well…"

"War?"

"I haven't had the full briefing yet," Cain said. "But yes. The Jumjul have openly declared war, and the Eeri have joined them."

"What?" I asked, feeling the walls of the tent closing in. "You're kidding, right? Tell me that's a joke or Miles put you up to that or something."

"I'm hurt you'd think I would joke about something like that." Miles sniffed.

I ignored that. "What about Lio? Any updates from him and the *Samaritan*?"

"Lio broke protocol." Miles held up his hand. "I know. But he had good reason. The *Samaritan* needed more work than we thought, which forced Lio to head to one of the Aligned Worlds trading hubs." He threw Cain a look. "Right now, Chancellor Heron is doing her best to keep supplies flowing, helping out where she can. She hasn't officially thrown in with any other faction. From what Lio told me, he should be here within the next few days. Once the repairs were completed, he was going to pick up your Master Glipglow and head our way, ideally with some reinforcements, if his contacts came through."

The master. I wondered if the information he'd found was obsolete now. Or if his work would reveal another unexpected part to all of this. I really hoped not. Even the universe had its hands full right then, with war breaking out. I didn't think either one of us needed another bombshell.

"Give us a minute?" Miles asked.

I realized he was addressing Cain and that Cain hadn't moved. *<Go ahead. It's okay. I'm okay.>*

Cain stood, gave Miles a rather nasty look, and left the tent.

"Killing someone isn't supposed to be easy," Miles said. He'd leaned forward in his chair and was staring at me. "You live with the memories for the rest of your life. And for someone like you, they'll haunt you unless you can come to terms with what happened. You've defended yourself and others before. This situation isn't any different"—I opened my mouth to protest—"blood relations or not. Just because they're called family doesn't automatically make them good people. Believe me, I know. From both sides of the coin. But right now, I need you to push everything you're feeling to the side. My people are trying to contact the Jumjul and see how we can come to some type of arrangement. And I will need you to stand witness to what happened—perhaps even a little more than that."

"And I'm supposed to take advice from a madman? Become someone like you?"

Miles winced and leaned back.

"How are you any different from Lucas?"

That got a reaction. And it wasn't a fair comparison, but my mind was still working on that blasted jigsaw puzzle.

"I'm nothing like him," Miles growled. "I don't murder entire planets, killing millions upon millions of innocent people. It's a fine line and maybe not even that. But what I do ensures smooth operations within my business and keeps the truly nightmarish from taking over."

"Oh, please. Now, you're trying to tell me you're some type of hero?"

<Mahia. Perhaps now isn't the time—>

<You're going to defend him? You?> I snapped. Pain or no pain, I got up off the cot and stormed out of the tent. Cain was standing off to one side but didn't come after me. My pesky mind knew I wasn't really upset with either of them. *I do have a point about Miles, though.* My emotions were cascading into chaos as I tried to process everything I'd just learned. *I died. Here. And the only reason I'm walking around is because of the Third.*

"You're right. I've killed and will do so again. I'm not the hero, and I'm not a good guy," Miles said as he walked up next to me.

"Then why are you here?"

He paused. "Because I want answers, just like you. I want to know what everyone has been so jumped up about. And like it or not, I've taken a liking to you."

"I don't consider that a compliment," I said.

"Yes, you do. Give it time," Miles replied.

After a rather uncomfortable silence, Miles shrugged and walked off. Cain eventually took his place.

"I thought I was prepared for the answers," I mumbled.

"There's no need to explain. What do you want to do next?"

What do I want? Or perhaps need? I looked up at the sky and pictured the blackness of space beyond Epo-5. *What else was out there? Cain and I could leave, just forget everything and walk away. Miles was smart and had resources. He could figure the rest out. We could let the IGJ know Lucas was dead, and maybe that would give them the leverage they needed to break up the Sun Worshipers. That was their problem anyway, not mine.*

I looked down at my hands and realized someone had put a new suit on me. "You?" *Please say yes.*

"Yes. After the med techs took a look at you. And here…" He reached into one of the pockets on his suit and pulled out the pendant, its amber color a dull reflection of what I saw shining with concern in Cain's eyes. "I didn't think you'd want anyone else to handle it."

I took it, undid part of the suit, and slipped the pendant around my neck. I didn't quite understand the rush of emotions or sentimentality that overtook me as I closed my suit. *<Thanks.>*

I stretched my fingers as wide as they could go, holding them there and feeling the pinpricks of pain between each finger. I was alive because of the Third. It had granted me the greatest gift of all. If I walked away, I would be walking away from it as well. I didn't think I could live with myself if I did that.

"We finish this. I want to go back down in the tunnels. Lucas has Wats's journal entries from when he talks about how I found another entrance, along with something about fabrication chambers. He was looking for something specific on Epo-5, the same thing I'm betting Lucas was hoping I'd lead him to, because after everything happened to us as kids, it sounds like Wats was a little light on the information. And I'm guessing it's what will help the Third. We find it and do what needs doing, then we're out of here."

Cain nodded and started to walk off but stopped and turned back to look at me. "He is still your father."

"Just like Lucas is still my brother? I'm not sure I claim either one of them anymore."

"Mahia, stop."

I froze but didn't turn around. *<I don't want to do this. Not now—not ever.>*

"You need to, or else you won't be able to move on." Cain moved to stand behind me and wrapped his arms around my shoulders. *<Do you remember when I told you that how we handle our fears is what matters? Not letting them devour us?>*

<Yes.>

<Don't let this fear devour you. What happened doesn't change who you are. And it doesn't change who he was. He's always been the same person—xenologist, Sun Worshiper, father, husband. It's the same with Lucas. You might not have known the total sum of both of them, but that knowledge doesn't change anything. It merely reveals another layer. Just as what happened here, to you, doesn't change who you are—it only reveals something else. But if you choose to let those feelings, those fears, take over, then that will change you. We all have a mixture of good and bad. Don't let the fear allow the bad to take over.>

<When did you get so wise?>

"I've always been wise. You've just been a tad too bullheaded to see it," Cain whispered.

That made me laugh. "You wouldn't know what to do with me if I was any other way."

<*True.*>

I watched the activity of Miles's team. They'd set up a temporary camp a few meters away from the one I'd woken up in. I counted roughly five different tents, with one more in the middle, at least triple the size. Parked next to that tent were a handful of rovers, and beyond the camp, two individuals were standing off by themselves.

"Is that…?"

Cain sighed and let go of me. "Yes. Miles held up his end of the bargain. He's brought the Star Eaters."

17

All the Moving Parts

"More like the Star Eaters found me," Miles said when we caught up with him.

The largest tent turned out to be the command center, with a few tables tucked off into a corner as a makeshift mess hall. Everyone was checking equipment and reporting to Miles, who was relishing being in command.

He moved to one of the tables and gestured for the two of us to sit. "Drinks? Food? The tent filters out the worst of the radiation. You can lift the masks on your suits and eat or drink in here."

I was going to decline but stopped. "Did you bring your chef?"

Miles grinned and snapped his fingers. "Three plates and hot tea." His chef, who'd been standing in the corner, bowed and got to work.

"You're absurd," I said.

"But you like it, don't you? Come on, admit it."

"I'll admit quality food goes a lot longer than zips," I said with a glance at Cain. "But back to the Star Eaters."

I was becoming concerned by how easily Miles was

switching from jovial madman to serious commander. And the serious commander was winning.

"They were waiting for me. I've got friends in all sorts of places, stashes for emergencies and the like. After I left the *Samaritan*, I headed to the nearest one, and lo and behold, there they were, patiently waiting for me to show up—no explanations, just confirmation of who I was and where we were headed. And they didn't say a thing on the ride over."

"Tipped off?" Cain asked.

"No, I don't think so. Who would've done that?"

"Lucas," Cain offered next then reconsidered. "But if he had an in with the Star Eaters, why not just go to them?"

"So, likely not Lucas," Miles said.

I mulled over the idea as the chef brought our plates. Each was piled high with steaming mounds of delicious-looking food. But as I stared at it, the thin strands of pasta morphed into the tendrils of darkness from the tunnel. I pushed the plate away, and both Miles and Cain shared a concerned look.

"Something else, then?" Miles asked.

"No. The tea will do it for now. Thanks," I said. "I don't think you were tipped off."

"What makes you say that?" Miles asked around a mouthful of the pasta.

"I think the Star Eaters have been watching me. Look, we know Wa... Pops"—I glanced at Cain—"was in contact with them. When the Star Eaters rescued me on the *Rapscallion*, they told me that they'd made a vow or something to him. The implication was that it

was something to do with me. And then my lawyers
have this letter from Pops but can't release it until they
hear from the Celestial Light, a.k.a. the Star Eaters. So
if they knew what was going on, I'm not surprised."

"Then the question is why," Miles said.

"This whole journey has been a huge old why. That
or the universe is giving me the—"

"We've just received word, sir," a woman said as
she stepped up to our table. "The Jumjul have received
your message and are demanding proof."

"Good. A step toward averting total disaster, then.
Any updates from Johnson or Poy-Ult?"

The woman shook her head. "Not yet, sir."

"Damn. Send Fox out to check on them. And tell
them if they don't have something for me within the
next hour, I'm going to be leaving them here."

I raised an eyebrow, but Miles shrugged. "Incentive.
They know I follow through."

"And what's so important?" I asked.

When Miles looked at Cain before answering, I
realized what that look meant. "Did you just ask him
for permission?"

"Yes, he did."

"Did I slip into an alternative universe or
something?"

Neither one of them laughed.

"Johnson is at the site. Where you shot Lucas. Trying
to find confirmation."

"Of what?" I growled.

"If Lucas is truly dead."

"And what would make you think otherwise?" I

looked down at my cup of tea, the steam still wafting up off the dark-brown liquid.

"There wasn't a body," Cain answered. "Blood, yes. And obvious signs of a struggle. But what we don't know is if Lucas did actually die or if Shelia and the others got to him in time."

I closed my eyes, not liking the warring emotions stirring inside me. "And how are they going to figure it out?"

"Johnson is checking the site for any clues, the amount of blood loss and the like. And Poy-Ult is searching for the Sun Worshipers' nest."

"But they're on the *Justus*," I began.

Cain shook his head. "No. There's no one there. Whatever Lucas and his followers did, they stripped the ship."

"I've got people working on that," Miles said.

"Okay, now I'm lost."

"When I got into orbit, we immediately brought up shields and were prepared to go into a full-on fight with the *Justus*. Which, by the way, was the only ship we detected in orbit or even close to Epo-5. But the *Justus* never fired. Nothing. So we went on a little expedition. The whole ship is empty, the overdrive engine smashed, and the bridge a disaster zone. The first order of business is trying to reestablish life support. Then my crew will go from there."

"And Yilmaz? Dr. Ashter? Are they really down here, then?"

"As far as we can tell, yes. I was tempted to reach out to them but decided to wait and see what you'd learned," Miles said.

"Oh, how thoughtful," I replied with as much sarcasm as I could muster.

"Just for that," Miles said and reached out to snag my plate as he'd just finished his own. "So, what's next?"

"I need to know about Lucas." I looked over at Cain. "But, Miles, you can stay on top of that. Is Ochoa awake?"

"She is," Miles answered then narrowed his eyes. "Why?"

"Because Cain's going to check in with her. I want the two of you to consider what Yilmaz might be up to. Consider our options." I wasn't oblivious to Cain's pained expression or the irritation through our connection. *<I'm sorry to ask this of you. But the two of you are former IGJ. And she was intelligence. And I trust her, and I definitely trust you. I want honest opinions, ones I can count on.>*

"And you?" Cain asked.

"I'm going to go have a chat with the Star Eaters."

Miles dropped his fork. "Oh, no. You don't get to have all the fun by yourself. I've been waiting for this moment for years."

I pushed the chair back and stood. "Then you'll have to wait a bit longer."

Cain waited until we were out of the tent to stop me. "I'm not going to let you go by yourself," he growled.

"I need to do this on my own." I pressed a hand against his chest. *<I know that probably sounds messed up after everything I've said and felt. But you're right about the fear. I can't let it eat away at me. And we don't have time. Right now, we need to divide and conquer. Lucas kept talking about*

a deadline. I don't know what that means yet, but we've got to cover all our bases.>

His eyes were twin sparks of emerald as he regarded me. But what I was coming to love about Cain was his ability to know when to stand his ground and when to let me stand mine.

"At the first sign of distress, though," he said.

"Of course. And Cain? I am sorry to have to ask this of you."

"No. If I'm asking you to face your fear, then I should be able to face my own." He leaned forward and touched his forehead to mine. *<Be careful.>*

<I'm only walking a few meters away.>

<All the same...>

We pulled back, and Cain turned and jogged off. *Time to go see a Star Eater. On purpose.*

18

Communication Breakdown

The Star Eaters hadn't moved from where I'd first spotted them. I took my time, trying to come up with a zinger of an opening question. They didn't move as I approached, not even a ripple among the dark-blue robes. *Maybe they're decoys.* I tried to lighten my mood, but that only made me take a sharp look at the ground, for the Third pushing through the dirt.

"Offspring of Wats Hawking Orion. Join us." The voice was gravelly and distorted, but I understood it well enough. With a deep breath and a lot of false bravado, I stepped up to stand next to the one on the left. I stood there and felt like a fool, all my questions having vanished except for one.

"How did you know Wats?"

"Do you now see with the Eye of Radiance?" the Star Eater countered.

"If you're asking if I understand what's going on, that's a resounding no."

They turned toward each other and shared a few clicks and whistles. *Just like on the* Rapscallion. *Was it their language or simply a vocal disguise?* The question sparked an idea. I crouched down—fortunately, we were standing on a patch of dirt—and drew the image of the three orbs with connecting lines.

"The Ray of Confluence."

Huh. Well, blow me over. I drew the symbol of the two squares.

"The Ray of Requirement."

So I drew the last symbol I'd seen in my vision, the circle with the herringbone pattern.

The Star Eater who'd been talking to me hissed and let out a series of sharp trills. It turned to face its companion. Alarmed, to say the least, I stood and took several steps back.

"The Vow upon the Celestial Plain has been broken." The Star Eaters turned toward me, their hands moving to their hoods.

"I don't think so." I closed my eyes and turned away from the pair. I was pretty sure they tried to blind me, but even if I hadn't been up-to-date on their little bag of tricks, it wouldn't have mattered. The ground shook, and I felt something brush up against me. I might have let out a little squeak of surprise as I peeked over my shoulder at what was going on.

A solid wall of the Third had exploded out of the ground between us. *Thanks?* I was oscillating between gratitude and freshly remembered fear.

<I'm coming.> Cain was jogging out of the make-shift camp toward me, and not too far behind was Miles.

<I'm all right. I think. Look familiar?>

Both men slowed as they inspected the wall of the Third. Miles in particular kept his distance.

"Are you sure it's the same?" he asked.

"Pretty sure," I replied with a quick glance at Cain. *<He doesn't know.>*

The Third shimmered then morphed into a triangle with rounded edges, and in the middle, it formed the symbol for the Ray of Requirement. On the other side of the Third, the Star Eaters bowed.

"We have traveled on a Ray of Absence, offspring of Wats Hawking Orion. We did not know the union was complete."

The symbol—no, the Third—appeared to melt and be absorbed back into the ground. Appearances could be deceiving, but it certainly looked as if the Third was in charge.

"First, let's clear the air. I haven't broken a vow because I didn't make a vow. Wats evidently did but not me."

"Are you not his offspring?"

All right, I see what you're getting at. "Yes. But if you're implying his vow extends to me, then you're going to have to fill me in because he failed to, on that front."

After one click, a pause was followed by a low whistle in response from the Star Eater.

"These words were spoken amongst the Celestial Plain." After a pause, Pops's voice came from the Star Eater, to my horror. "Protect my offspring, Mahia Eimariana Orion, and I shall ensure she is there for the Ray of Ascension."

Voice disguiser it is, then. "And what exactly is this Ray of Ascension?"

"The Ray of Confluence reformed."

Clear as waste fuel. "And what's that?"

The Star Eaters knelt and drew two identical symbols in the dirt—the first one I'd drawn with the three orbs.

I shook my head. "We've established that. But what does it mean? Does the symbol break down into something else? What is this?" I moved as close as I dared and pointed at one of the orbs with my boot.

"The Ray of Confluence."

Fine. I knelt next to them and erased everything but one orb. "What does this mean?"

"There is no Ray."

"Okay, that's not getting me anywhere." I erased the remaining orb and tried again. "Show me the Ray of Ascension."

Together, as if sharing one mind, the Star Eaters once again drew in the dirt. That time, it was a spiral with one small orb at the center and another at the end of the spiral.

"What about the third orb?" I asked. When I didn't receive an answer, I stood and dusted off my hand. "Then why do I need to be present at this Ray of Ascension?"

The Star Eaters stood as well. "To feed the One."

"Excuse me?"

"The offspring of Wats Hawking Orion must be at the Ray of Ascension to ensure the One, from which sprang the Two, has been fed."

And I'm out.

No, I wasn't, really. But I was completely lost and not liking the implications. "Okay. Hold that thought." I turned to Cain and Miles. "All right, the two of you have any great insights here?"

"Maybe," Miles said. "But I need to double-check something first. I'll be back." Before I could stop him, he darted off.

"I never worked a case associated with the Star Eaters. But even then, they're not the same, correct?" Cain asked.

"That's what Dr. Ashter implied. And despite his less-than-stellar trust record, I'm confident he was telling the truth there."

"Back to my first question, then," I said, addressing the pair. "When did you first meet Wats?"

The one who hadn't spoken yet did. "On the world of a failed union."

I was beginning to lose my patience. I could've used a healthy dose of first-contact training in patience. Technology and AI translation programs definitely helped in those situations, but even the best tech wasn't able to pick up on the thousands of minute variations, cultural references, and the like. First-contact teams were probably some of the most unsung heroes out there. If I made it through all this alive—and provided the rest of the known worlds did as well—I wanted to remember to donate some credits to some training programs.

Thank goodness for Cain, who stepped in to help. "As per the Accords of Filin, the majority of the known worlds recognize this year as time-stamped at 2623. Do you as well?"

<Why didn't I think of that?>

Cain was good. His face remained neutral, but I felt a rush of smugness through our connection.

<Thank my mother and her insistence at diplomacy training.>

"Yes, we can."

"Can you tell me then, in reference to the Accords of Filin, what was the time stamp when you first met Wats Hawking Orion?"

After a brief pause, the first Star Eater said, "The year 2604."

"Thank you," Cain said with a small nod of respect. "Mahia?"

Twenty-six oh four. That was… good grief, nineteen years ago. Now, that makes me feel old.

"Twenty-six oh four… That would've been when he worked on Est-E-24, I think. Yeah, I'm pretty sure that's right."

"Would that make sense?"

The connections I was beginning to make certainly did. "Est-E-24. The IGJ commissioned a group of forensic scientists, archaeologists, and recovery specialists to work on that world. Pops was hired because of his impeccable record. He was many things, but he was at least good at his job. Something about the IGJ wanting to figure out what had happened to a once-thriving colony." I took a hard look at the Star Eaters. "Are you telling us that what happened to the colony is connected to you? The Third?"

The Star Eaters both bowed toward us in response.

That added a whole other dimension to what was going on with Dar. "Were we wrong? Surely not, though.

I mean"—I looked at Cain—"the Third wanted to be free, right?"

"From what you've shared, yes. Whatever the Third might have been trying to do, on Dar at least, the relationship took a sour turn. To put it mildly. The Darquets exploited and abused the relationship, or else I do not believe they would have prevented it from being able to get to its ship."

His reasoning made sense, thank goodness. "No, you're right."

"Tell me more about Est-E-24," Cain said.

I frowned. "There's really not much I can tell you. I don't know details. We'll have to look it up. But I know Pops worked on some mass graves, trying to identify them and see if the remains held any clues as to what had happened to them. But now, I'm guessing he had a vague idea and was looking for confirmation."

"As was the IGJ, I would presume," Cain added.

I addressed the Star Eaters once more. "Can you tell me why Wats reached out to you?"

"He did not initiate a Ray of Inquiry."

Thank goodness that ray sounded straightforward. "Then who did?"

"Commandant Earon Seli-Lut."

The name sounded familiar, but I wasn't bringing up any details. <*You?*>

"Commandant Seli-Lut was the commandant of the IGJ before Yilmaz took over," Cain said.

19

Connections or Herrings

"So it wasn't just Yilmaz following what Pops and the others were working on but the IGJ as well," I said.

"Or he was a part of the Sun Worshipers, and Yilmaz was cleaning up a mess he'd made," Cain offered.

Those were two very plausible explanations. *There was something she said about cleaning up a mess, wasn't there?* But I couldn't recall the details. My intuition told me Yilmaz and her quest had more going on than just picking up where the previous commandant had stopped. Even if she was making sure nothing blew back on the IGJ for whatever might have happened, I'd gotten the impression something in the mix was personal for her as well.

"Is there anything you can remember from the IGJ that would shed some light on this?" I asked.

Cain didn't answer right away. "No, but Ochoa might."

In my frustration at communicating with the Star Eaters, I'd forgotten what I'd sent Cain off to do. "How is she?"

"Holding it together. They want to send her up to

the ship, but she won't have it. Typical bravado that she's seen worse."

"Found it," Miles interrupted us. He rushed up to us like a little kid having made the greatest discovery in the world. "I was right. Just needed to double-check. Pola Tahh. The Capsa tree. One of the most popular myths surrounding the tree was that it was a gift from the One, from which sprang the Two." He waggled his eyebrows at me, and I tried hard not to laugh at his ridiculous expression.

The Star Eaters interrupted. "It was a Ray of Reverence."

"Excuse me?" I asked. "What was?"

"The gift to the One, from which sprang the Two."

I stared at them in disbelief. "You're saying the capsa tree was a gift?" My brain's little reactor exploded into a million different pieces. "To you? From Pola Tahh?"

"No, that's not possible," Miles tried to interject. "Genetically——"

I held up a hand and shushed him. "How many of you are there?" I asked. "Star E—no, the Celestial Light."

"We are the Two from which was the One."

"That's it? No more?" Miles was catching on. "Just the pair of you? Throughout thousands of years, all those sightings, just you two?"

"We are the Two from which was the One."

Cain gently grabbed my arm and pulled me off to the side. "I agree with Miles. That claim doesn't make sense. How could these two be the same for all that time?" he murmured.

I shook my head and stared past him in wonderment

at the Star Eaters. *I really need to correct myself. The Celestial Plain. Or perhaps the Two.* "Can you honestly tell me we know everything there is to know about the universe? That all the nooks and crannies have been explored?"

If not for Cain's suit, that would've been the perfect tail-twitching moment. "Of course not. But this defies what we do know of how things work."

"Of how what works, exactly? Physics? Different dimensions? All the different alien species that might be out there? What about beyond our galaxy?" I pressed. "Cain, if there's one thing I've come to realize in these past few months, it's that what we think we know is true definitely isn't."

He moved a hand as if to run it through his hair. When he realized what he was doing, he scowled and dropped his arm. I couldn't help but grin. I knew he wasn't satisfied, and if I'd been in his shoes, I probably would've been just as skeptical. And even though I'd shared my experiences with him, he hadn't been right there in those visions with me. I brushed past him and Miles.

"You're the beings made of light that I've seen, right?"

"We are the Two from which was the One. We are the keepers of the Celestial Light. We are the harvesters of the Rays. We stand as guardians to the Celestial Plain."

"And the Third?"

"They are the great Gatherer, the lights that illuminate the Path Maker. They are the Caretakers."

"Sir, pardon the interruption." One of Miles's men was walking toward us.

I heard him speaking but was staring in awe at the

Two. *Celestial Light? Harvesters? This is getting confusing. Let's just stick with "the Two" for now.*

"What is it?" Miles asked, dreamy wonder in his own voice.

I thought it would be safe to say we'd uncovered something none of us had dreamed of in a million years.

"Johnson and Poy-Ult have reported in, sir."

"Mahia? Coming or staying?"

That was a tough decision. We were finally making headway with the Two, but I needed to know what Miles's people had found out. "Will you come with us?" I asked them.

The Two bowed, and one of them spoke. "No. We will wait here."

"And you won't leave? You'll stay right here?"

"A Vow will be made."

Seeing how stubbornly they'd stuck to the vow they'd made with my pops, I was satisfied—for the moment. "I'm coming, but Miles?"

"Yup, way ahead of you. Freddie, get someone out here to keep an eye on these two. No interference, just to keep tabs on them."

"Yes, sir."

As we walked back up to the campsite, I couldn't help but glance over my shoulder at the Two. They'd resumed their position, staring off toward the horizon—or at least I presumed they were staring. I had so many questions. *Do they have eyes? How do the robes work? They had to have been designed to contain the light they're made of. Did they make the cloth? And if not, who did?*

<I think there will be time enough for that, my little xenologist.>

I blushed but grinned at Cain. "It's just so exciting. And I bet Dr. Ashter doesn't even have a clue."

"I wouldn't be so sure of that," Miles said. Since we'd made it back to the main tent, he was already scanning through a stack of reports. "It looks like Yilmaz and the good Dr. Ashter have gone underground."

"What?" My little bubble of joy popped.

"We've been monitoring their site as well." Miles handed me the report.

His scout had been keeping tabs on the biosigns, and when several of them disappeared, the scout moved in for a closer look. With no indications of weapons fire, no one could account for why the biosigns would just wink out. But then the scout got a look inside their operation and determined a good number of Dr. Ashter and Yilmaz's team were moving their equipment underground, into a tunnel system.

Damn. Pops had said there was more than one entrance.

"We've got to get down there. Take the Two with us if they'll go. We need to find whatever is down there before Yilmaz and Dr. Ashter," I said and handed the report to Cain.

"Agreed. But first, update me on Johnson and Poy-Ult."

Freddie snapped to attention. "Yes, sir. Johnson has come to the reasonable conclusion that Lucas Orion didn't die. The blood loss and scattered debris led Johnson to determine that emergency aid was rendered and Lucas Orion transferred to another site."

Miles looked at me with a carefully controlled expression. "Do you know exactly where the shots hit him?"

"No," I said. I'd been so mixed up emotionally that I hadn't paid attention. "But he would be needing massive skin grafts. The sludge had—"

Miles jumped in. "No need for further details. I get the picture. What about Poy-Ult? Any luck there?"

Freddie shook his head. "No, sir. Poy-Ult is requesting permission to expand his radius. But so far, he hasn't found any energy signatures at all."

"He won't," Cain said.

"Why do you say—" Miles stopped himself. "They're underground as well."

"Logical conclusion."

"Freddie, get a team together. We're going to take a trip into the depths of Epo-5."

"Yes, sir," Freddie replied and hurried off, already barking orders at the other men and women in the tent.

"I brought along some reinforced, cutting-edge military-grade suits," Miles told us. "I suggest we get changed. And outfitted. I don't think we're going to be sitting down to tea with our friends."

"Agreed," I said. "I'll change then go talk to the Two. We need them as well."

20

Epo-5 May Not Be Unique

The suits Miles had brought didn't look or feel different from the previous ones, and I was a little suspicious about the "cutting-edge" part. But if Miles was going to be wearing one of them, then I doubted I had too much to worry about. Cain joined me, but we changed in silence. As I slipped on the hood and turned on the suit—its nanofibers sealed the suit into one solid piece—I couldn't help but wonder about Pops and the choices he'd made. I'd been so angry with him after listening to those journal entries, but since my anger had cooled—somewhat—I could clearly think about how he'd decided he had wanted me to have a normal life. *Perhaps you really cared.* But the underlying action and reaction was that Pops had turned his focus toward Lucas. *Would I have become like Lucas if Pops hadn't tried to bury my memories?*

A part of me wanted to get stuck on the question, to allow anger and frustration to overtake me. Those were easy emotions and ones I was far more familiar with than trying to stay calm and let myself move past the hard stuff to the quick answer. Much like staying in hiding—being a recluse had prevented me from getting hurt, or so I'd thought.

As the suit alerted me that it was finished and ready to go, I took a deep breath. *I am not my brother. Nor am I my father. I am me. Our choices and actions are our own. I am not responsible for my father or my brother.*

"Ready?" Cain asked.

"Yup, let me go get the Two, and you get our ride."

Miles was more than prepared, and I was impressed. Not only had he brought the tents, suits, and personnel, but he'd brought land rovers. *Beats hiking in this place.* I would've had a ball with one as a kid. *It's probably a good thing they weren't as accessible then.*

As I walked back toward the Two, who hadn't moved from their spot, I wondered why they'd chosen Epo-5 or any of the other planets Pops had talked about. *Was there something special about each one? Or were they just random choices? Or maybe they didn't have a choice.* I was beginning to believe something catastrophic had occurred. If I was interpreting my visions correctly, the Two *and* the Third had all either lived together at one time or, at the very least, worked together. To what purpose, I didn't have a clue. But I highly doubted their separation was by choice. *Or something forced them apart.*

I waved at the man standing off to the side, monitoring them. He gave me a curt nod but didn't leave. *Good man.*

The Two turned toward me as I approached.

"I need you to come with me. If you can help us understand what it is that's down there, maybe we can get to it before anyone else does. And you can help me know how exactly I'm supposed to be helping the Third."

"We cannot. We have made a vow and will not move from this spot."

Whoops. Should have tumbled to the fact of how literal these guys were. "That vow is fulfilled. You haven't moved, and I've returned. So now, I need your help. I've made a promise—which I'm guessing you're aware of—to the great Gatherer. But I can't do this alone."

"We cannot."

Breathe—just breathe.

"The union has been completed. The knowledge is inside—"

I held up a hand. "Nope. Don't say it. That's too cliché."

The Two turned toward each other for a rather fast-paced exchange of clicks and whistles.

"When the Ray of Ascension has been revealed, then shall the Two who sprang from the One be."

I tried a few more times, but the Two actually ignored me. *Fine. Just fine and dandy and Saturn's rings thrown in together.* At least they'd told me what they did. One thing I was sure of was that whatever we were looking for was called the Path Maker. That could mean so many different things. Nobody knew if the Two were translating their language or concepts accurately. If they were as old as they implied, then I certainly hoped they'd become linguistic experts after all that time, just cryptic in nature. *Like so many seem to enjoy being.*

I trudged back to the campsite and found Cain

waiting with one of the land rovers. "You know how to drive one of those things?"

He looked affronted and motioned for me to get in. "Miles already left. They're about fifteen minutes ahead of us."

He started the land rover, and we took off. Despite Cain's assurances, I questioned if he'd actually driven one before and was grateful for the seat belts and handholds.

Reaching the base of the foothills where Lucas and I had climbed took a little over an hour. I didn't pay too much attention, since Cain was taking a little more care in maneuvering the vehicle. The rover had a dashboard with a ton of different readouts, and Cain turned on the protective shielding to prevent us from getting splattered by goo when the rover hit any soft rocks.

"Oh, fudge nuggets," I said and sat up. "I forgot to grab—"

"Nope. Check your pack," Cain said, finding a way around a particularly large boulder.

I leaned forward, dug into the pack at my feet, and pulled out Lucas's palm pad. "What would I do without you?" I felt a rush of pride and smugness from him. *<Thanks, Cain.>*

Lucas had probably memorized everything on the palm pad. I knew I would've. But I didn't have time to go back and start at the beginning. I needed to pick up where I'd left off. If Lucas was on a timetable, then so were we. *If only I knew why.*

Time stamp 2596.3.30:

"I've been assured that Mahia's vitals are normal

and that there should be no lasting side effects of radiation poison. But Dr. Lumen doesn't have an explanation for how she survived. Could it be there's something we've missed within her genetics? Something she has that Lucas lacks? Because Lucas wasn't as lucky. He'll require several rounds of treatment and some reconstructive work. I've asked for multiple samples to be taken from Mahia, and I'll start working on them right away. I need to understand the difference, and Lucas will have to start training.

"If only Mahia could tell me what happened. But she's still refusing to talk. And I've made my decision."

I fast forwarded here and there, not really interested in listening to him discuss that part.

Time stamp 2596.4.7:

"Lucas is back home, and it appears both he and Mahia are picking up their relationship where they left off. Lucas is too young to fully understand what happened, but I have noticed he seems to be challenging her a bit more.

"We've resumed work, and I've kept the teams away from where we found Mahia. I don't know how she got inside the tunnels, but at this point, I don't think that's going to be relevant—for now. It's a question I am hoping to revisit. I've expanded the team's areas to include the eastern edge of where Mahia must have been. I've got Milo on a scouting route, and I'll follow up by myself before having the teams move forward.

"There have been a significant number of glyphs that appear to be unique to Epo-5, and even though we've tried multiple translation programs, we're still up against a dead end there. We do know what we're seeing is a mix of Star Eater symbols and what the indigenous population must have turned into their own expressions of what they believed was going on here—more than likely some type of religious ideology. I'm reluctant to ask, but I believe Mrs. Gol is going to need to be looped in on those discoveries. We can add the images into our database and go from there."

Time stamp 2596.4.9:

"We've scouted the caverns we have access to, and so far, no signs they were fabrication chambers or anything like the alpha fragments we've been working off of. Nor have there been any remains. I'd expected to find mass graves at least, given previous discoveries. But so far, we're not finding anything to indicate the local population was killed off due to contact with the Star Eaters or the machine. So the question that has to be asked is if something different happened here.

Did they never fully initiate contact? Was contact successful? But if so, what happened?"

"Machine?" Cain asked.

I hit Pause. "In what I've listened to, he hasn't said anything about a machine before. But that would line up with whatever a fabrication chamber might be for."

"Keep going," Cain said.

"I'm still hopeful we'll find an intact specimen here, that the reason we're not finding the mass graves is because contact was indeed successful. We know the machine and its value. But we need the last bit of information on how to interface with it. If we can find that, then everything we've worked toward, sacrificed for, will have a purpose. And I know Hopper is going to contradict me on this. No, the tunnel of bones isn't what we're looking for. Those were laid out with reverence and mimicked the Star Eater glyphs. So that was created after the population became aware of the Star Eaters. But whether or not that's from a first-contact situation or another influence, we can't know. The bones' scans are not showing any of the genetic profiles we're after."

I stopped the recording. "So, they're looking for a machine. But one that does what?"

"Lucas has demonstrated he has the power to destroy an entire planet."

"No," I said. "If that was the same device or machine

or weapon or whatever, then why would they be here? Why would he need me? I've got to believe those are two separate issues."

Cain stayed quiet, and I stared out at the desolation of Epo-5. First contact with any species is always a toss of the dice. A thousand different problems could rise up within minutes—miscommunication on so many different levels. The Two and the Third—*there had to be a translation issue there*—were not easy to understand. If they had been explorers and tried to initiate first contact, everything could've gone horribly wrong. *But on multiple worlds?* If that idea was true, then they were not able to adapt. *No, I don't think so.* What I'd seen and what I knew contradicted that. If the Two really were as old as they'd implied, then they would have to be extremely adaptable. *I mean, come on, it took me a while to get used to the idea of neon jumpsuits and feathered hair.* But I wasn't confessing I was ever swept up in that fashion trend.

The Third had to adapt on Dar whether they wanted to or not. So the ability to adapt had to be within their skill set. *If that's the case, then did they simply not care?* That much more chilling idea would, unfortunately, fit with what I'd seen, at least from the Two. But from the Third, I wanted to believe in some kind of compassion within, or at least empathy. But drawing that conclusion from my limited time of interacting with the Third was sketchy.

I skipped ahead to another journal entry, time stamp 2596.4.15:

"We've come across a dead end—several, in fact, on a variety of levels. While I still have several months left on Epo-5, funding is being diverted elsewhere. It turns out the emperor has his sights set on expanding the trade relations with the Eeri. And Mrs. Gol and the director are supporting this. I know they've long believed there are answers within Eeri-controlled space but have always been denied access."

The rover came to a dead stop.

"Repeat that," Cain said. We listened again, and Cain sat back in his seat. "There's no record of the emperor being involved with the Eeri. Starbase 9.2, or rather Kel Station, was built in 2591 with the support of the Telt, the Eeri, and…" He paused, trying to remember.

"The Goldsmith Consortium," I supplied.

"Right. So how does the emperor or the Sun Worshipers fit into all that?"

"I highly doubt in a good way," I muttered as Cain started the rover again. "How far out are we?"

"About twenty minutes."

21

Are You in or Out?

Miles was issuing directions by the time we got there. Everyone was scurrying around and setting up a few small tents and a ton of gear. Cain stopped, and one of the men walked over and told him where to park. I couldn't believe my eyes. The area had been cleared. The three strange slabs of rock with the glyphs remained, but the rest of the area had been cleaned up.

As I climbed out of the rover, Miles came bouncing over. "Pretty good, huh?"

"How?" I asked, dumbfounded.

"I hire only the best," he said with a wink. "We've got the area cleared out and will be setting up another campsite, since we're not sure how long we'll be here. I've also got two teams working on establishing a modulating force field, one designed to work as a filtration system to help cut down on the levels of radiation, and the other to help repel any nasty creatures that might come sniffing around."

"Seems like a bit of overkill," Cain commented. "Just putting up a gigantic sign announcing where we're at."

Miles grinned and not kindly. "Let them come. I've been working toward this too. And I'm going to be the first one to get to the prize."

"Miles," I said, "you need to pop all those little hopeful schemes of yours. Because if you think you're going to be getting something useful out of this, besides helping me, then you might as well lock me up or shoot me or something. I'm not helping you so you can lay claim to what's down there or use it for your own nefarious purposes."

The little scuttle crab had the good graces to at least appear affronted. "I wouldn't dream of it."

I took a step closer and looked him in the eye. "I mean it, Miles. I appreciate everything you've done—I really do—putting aside how you go about some of that. But this is the line where you need to step up and commit to me and me alone, or else you can take all your fancy gear and people and leave."

I heard the breath Cain sucked in and could feel him coil, ready to fight or flee, whatever we needed to do, depending on what Miles decided.

Then Miles did the one thing I least expected. He pulled me in for a big hug. "There she is. There's the Orion I knew was inside you."

"Take your hands off her," Cain growled.

Miles did and stepped back.

Was that a compliment or an underhanded dig? Either way, it still didn't answer my question. "So, are you in or out?"

Miles bowed with a flourish. *He should've added a cape to his suit. That would fit his over-the-top style.* "I am in. I have always been in," he said as he straightened. "My dear, Mahia. I may ensure things go my way or add to my already substantial vaults, but there is one piece of training I've retained from my childhood, whether any of my family took it to heart or not. There is a balance of power within the universe, which must be maintained, where neither good nor bad can fully take control, because one does not exist without the other."

"Or those who can exploit such an idea," Cain said.

Miles winked. "Perhaps." Then he reached out, took my hand, and touched it to his forehead. "But I will make a promise to you. Whatever is down there, I will leave it to you to decide what is to be done. I am merely here as an instrument you can use." He let go, and a boyish grin spread across his face. "But for the love of Pluto, at least let me look at it. This whole quest has been driving me batty for years."

His promise was as good as I was going to get.

"Perhaps," I replied with a sly smile of my own.

Miles clapped with excitement and started issuing orders again.

"He's still not trustworthy," Cain said as Miles practically pranced away.

"Is that an honest assessment or a judgment still clouded by the past?" I asked.

Flecks of dark emerald peppered his violet eyes as he regarded me. "Both."

I decided then wasn't the time to press and turned my attention back to the hustle and bustle instead. "So, I see how you guys were able to get to me." While the crews had left the three slabs of rock where they stood, they'd modified the one I'd mysteriously run through.

"Yes, you should see what we found," Cain said.

We moved through the crowd of workers, and I couldn't help but admire the efficiency of the whole operation. It reminded me of the Weplies. *Would even consider going back there once everything is said and done, if it wasn't for the death threat and all.*

"These are constructed from local rock formations, but they've been shaped and embedded with a level of technology I haven't seen. And I don't think Miles and his experts have either," Cain said and pointed toward where they'd cut an opening in the rock. "We tried explosives first—crude but should have done the job."

That explains the tremors I felt. "But it didn't?"

Cain shook his head. "Not enough, anyway. I still don't know what to make of Miles's timing, but he'd brought along a variety of tools. Ended up using a laser saw."

"That seems… strange. If the rock was designed to withstand explosives, you'd think that whoever constructed it would have considered that option too."

"At the time, I didn't care," Cain said, his eyes melting to pure amber. "All I knew was I had to get to you."

Lucky me. And I meant it. If not for Cain and our connection, I would still be trapped in the tunnels.

I reached out to touch the rock, and my hand passed right through it. "Should've seen that coming," I said and quickly withdrew my hand.

"At least it explains how you were able to get into the tunnels," Cain said with a curious expression. "Do it again, but off to the side of where we made the cut."

Though I wasn't keen on taking too many chances

of something malfunctioning and finding myself stuck inside a rock slab, I obliged. Cain moved to stand just outside the entrance and nodded. Slowly, I let one finger pass through the rock, then another, and finally my whole hand.

"Look," Cain said.

"Kind of hard to do," I replied but stretched to the side to try to see what he was seeing while praying I didn't lose my hand. "Oh. Huh."

The edges where the rock had been cut were glowing a soft blue. I withdrew my hand to get a closer look. The outside layer of rock was obvious, and wedged between was a thick, dark mass.

When I tentatively stretched out a finger, Cain grabbed my hand. "Is that wise?"

"You were the one who asked me to put my hand through the rock," I chided.

"That was a fairly known outcome."

"Really? And what great bundles of scientific evidence do you have telling you nothing would happen?" I asked.

Cain shrugged but released my hand.

<Thought so.>

But I could be a little more cautious. I let my finger hover a hair's width away from the core of the rock, but nothing happened. *Silly. What did you think was going to happen?* To be honest, I thought the Third—because I didn't know what else it might be—would stretch out and either touch my finger, make a few different geometrical designs, or at least glow. So I moved my hand and slid my fingers into the rock and was rewarded with a soft blue glow.

"The first time I was here, something swallowed me," I stated. "I know, but I don't have a better term at this point. It took me into the tunnels. But only after I'd injured myself. Did it choose me because I was hurt? Because I was dying? Lucas would've been in worse shape than I at that point."

"Perhaps when we discover what lies within, you'll find an answer to that," Cain suggested.

"Maybe. But it does make sense. I mean"—I waved at the big slab of rock—"with everything that's happened to me. The Two modified the smart bots because they knew what had happened to me, that I'd already made contact with the Third. And I'm also guessing that if you hadn't been injured and I was so hell-bent on going to Dar to save you, that the Two would have manipulated Miles even further to get me there. Or at least somewhere this 'union thing' could take place. And it also solves this mystery. Come on."

We stepped into the tunnel, and I found the nearest glyph. I had a brief moment of hesitation, but considering the amount of time I'd already spent in the tunnels, I was fairly certain—okay, maybe not that much, but I needed Cain to see—that taking my glove off for a split second wouldn't cause too much damage.

I laid my hand on the glyph and watched as it glowed softly. "Impressive, huh?"

Cain crossed his arms, not sharing my enthusiasm.

"What, no round of applause for my nifty little trick?" I asked.

<No. I don't like the implications. And I would prefer to put this whole matter to rest and ensure your safety.>

Heat rose to my cheeks, and I had to look away. <*Um, thanks.*> Realizing how much Cain meant to me and vice versa was still a little jarring.

"All right, you two little lovebirds," Miles said, striding toward us, "let's get moving. Time's a-wasting. And for Jupiter's sake, put your glove back on."

22

Nice Try

"Sir, we're not detecting any life signs within the next kilometer from Checkpoints B and C," a young woman reported to Miles, "with a second chamber appearing at the end of the offshoot tunnel from Checkpoint C"—she pointed at the holomap above Miles's palm pad—"here."

"Good, send your team out into the next kilometer block. Be careful," he ordered. "We're bound to meet up with one of the other groups sooner or later." He continued for my benefit without being asked a question, "We're mapping as we go, building off the data we extracted from your suit. We know the other entry point to be around where Yilmaz set up camp, but we're running blind when it comes to Lucas." He stopped and brought up a holo of the map so far, to point at it. "We've covered most of the tunnels, here and here. Is there anything we might have missed or that the suit didn't record correctly?"

Appreciating the information, I took my time to try

to recall where I'd been. "No, I don't think so. What about the bone tunnel?"

"Here. The bones extend for three meters, then we're back to the rock." He rotated the map. "Here's the chamber where the tunnel drops off. They've sent out an array of sensor bots to see what we can find out about the big chamber. From what I'm seeing—" he switched to another display—"we're looking at about twenty percent of the area that's been mapped so far." He tucked the palm pad back into his pack. "We're going to have to make a choice here. I can send out teams to scout, but ultimately, whatever is down here, you're going to have to find it. If it was that easy, then the others would've nabbed it and gotten off world by now."

With a deep breath, I considered my options. Pops had talked about the fabrication chambers, which made me believe something could be learned there. *But was that the chamber I found? A fabrication chamber could be any number of things.*

But something was nagging at me, as though I knew what choice I should make, but the message was all scrambled up.

"Mahia?" Miles asked.

"Let her think," Cain growled.

Right. Come on. Put it together. Whatever the "machine" was, it was important, valuable, and hidden—worth protecting. *What do you do with something of value? You put it in a safety deposit box or hire a security firm to protect it. To guard it. Guardians. Caretakers. That was what the Two had talked about. And here was the Third on Epo-5, in the tunnels.*

So, a false wall? That would take forever, since I'm the only one who can walk through walls.

"You wouldn't have any tech on you to mimic what I can do, can you?" I half teased.

"I need specifications," Miles replied.

"To walk through the walls, seeing if there's any hidden treasures behind them," I said.

Miles didn't bat an eye. He actually thought about it but, in the end, shook his head. "Modifying the transportation tech would take too long, and we'd need to do extensive mapping first to make sure we weren't sending people into more solid rock."

"But that's what you're considering? A hidden area? Or chamber?" Cain asked me.

I nodded. "I mean… It kind of has to be, right? Or else why haven't they found anything yet?"

"I'll tell the teams to modify their scans," Miles said and moved off to start issuing a new set of orders.

<*What?*> Cain asked.

<*I still feel like I'm missing something. That I already know the answer. I need to walk.*> As he stayed a few steps behind me, I paced through the tunnels. *Everything has led to this planet. I'm sure of it. Or else why would Lucas and the others be here too? Pops obviously thought there was something here, so what do I know that he doesn't?*

I considered everything I could remember Mrs. Gol telling me and the less-than-fun conversations with Yilmaz, but nothing seemed to hint at what my subconscious was trying to dredge up. *The Holy One didn't say anything either. I'm sure of that. If there was any great secret to find within the Third, I highly doubt she would've casually dropped that. The only thing they seemed to know—that no one else had figured out—was how to communicate and use the Third. I cringed at the thought. How many years had the Darquets been forcing the Third to heal? What had that done to the Third? Wonder if that meant the Darquets had had to up the number of people they fed to the Third in order to keep it mollified.*

"Oh, I'm such an idiot," I said and took off.

"Miles!" Cain shouted as he took off after me.

I raced through the tunnels, checking where I was by using my suit. Soon, I skidded to a stop at the entrance of the bone tunnel.

"It's here. I know it." I ripped off my gloves and started touching the bones.

Miles had brought a few of his workers with him, and they started scanning the area. "Initial sweeps didn't detect anything. Are you sure?"

"Yes." But after a few minutes of touching random bones, nothing was happening. I stepped back. "The Third needs to feed, and on Dar, that was accomplished with the individuals they buried with it in that cavern. But that wasn't done out of reverence for the Third or the relationship—just a necessity in order to keep the Third alive and healing their people. But here, this is different. Pops had the answer but dismissed it. Whoever Hopper was, was right."

"Hopper?" Miles asked.

Cain shook his head.

I saw the apparent Star Eater glyphs, the ones Pops would have picked up on too. I scanned the walls again, and that time, I spotted it. Skillfully woven within the wall, the glyph wasn't immediately obvious. An observer needed to know what to look for.

"Here, this is it." I stepped forward, laid my hand on the bones in the middle of the pattern, and closed my eyes.

"If we're waiting for some kind of signal, I don't get it," Miles said.

I opened one eye then the other. *Yup—nothing.* "Damn. I was so sure."

<You spotted something no one else did. Keep looking. There might be something else.>

He was right. I couldn't give up just because I wasn't Miss Perfect with the right answer on the first try. I shook my hand—as if something about it was magical—and started looking again.

"Wait," Miles said. "You touched the bones but not the wall. What if that makes the difference?"

My eyes lit up. "That makes sense. Oh, I could hug you." When he opened his arms, I rolled my eyes. "Not literally."

Feigning hurt feelings, he shuffled forward and gave an experimental pull on a bone. "Hmm, we're going to need some help on this."

Cain moved forward and tried a few as well, but none of the bones budged.

"Makes sense, though. I mean, they're trying to protect it or keep it hidden," I said.

"It does, but I've got a feeling this could take some time. Do you want to wait here?" Cain asked.

I shrugged. "Why not? Unless you think there's something else I'm missing down here."

"I am curious about the fabrication chambers your father referenced. If he discusses those, then I'm assuming there's valuable intel there."

"Fair point. While they're working on this, why don't we scan through the rest of Pops's files, see what turns up?"

That turned out to be a great idea. Cain and I moved down the tunnel a bit, giving Miles and his crew room to work. Plus, I really didn't want random ears listening to what Pops had to say, not even Miles. I could fill him in with what he needed to know. Cain and I skimmed through several of the documents and listened to snippets here and there. Pops gave updates on the health of Lucas and me and discussed dwindling funds and how Silvia—Ms. Bettle—might be able to source what they needed through other means. I could tell by the tone of his voice that he was becoming discouraged even as he talked about working with Lucas.

Almost at the end of the time my family had spent on Epo-5, we hit an entry that caught our interest.

Time stamp 2596.2.25:

"We're a little over two months away from wrapping up work on Epo-5. On the surface, I believe I've reached a satisfying conclusion to the inconsistencies in the student's work. That information can be processed and presented right away. In regard to the work within the tunnels, despite my reminders to Mrs. Gol and the director that they've reduced our funding, both are unhappy with the small amount of progress I've made. And

I have questioned whether or not I should turn in the files concerning Mahia. But if I do that, now that we're several months past the incident, I know what the repercussions will be. And any leeway I might have garnered with how they handled her would be gone.

"I believe in the work we're doing—to be able to harness the power of the stars and to understand where the Star Eaters came from and what they want. But I don't give a crap about the purity nonsense Mrs. Gol and the others spout. We know—from the research done on Kibol 3 and what the Telt have provided—that the genetic maps are key, the key to the machine, not to mention the holy texts from Pola Tahh."

"At least he wasn't a purist," I said with a huge sigh of relief. I hadn't realized how much that was weighing on me until I heard him speak those words. "And talk about handing you what you need on a silver plate."

"What does silver have to do with it? Did I miss something?" Cain asked.

I laughed and shook my head. "Old Earth saying. Basically, we just got lucky and hit the jackpot of information. We know exactly where to look next to understand this whole thing."

"I see." The tone of Cain's voice said he didn't feel the same way.

<*So… what?*> I asked.

"The Telt? Do you really think they'll just let you

ask about their relationship with one of the most hated groups in the known worlds?" Cain said.

"And…?"

He narrowed his eyes and considered it. "Pola Tahh. You're thinking about their holy texts, then. But wouldn't Miles have that information? He is a collector of the Three Heralds."

I stared at Cain then slapped a hand to my forehead. "How stupid of me. Yes. Not only him but Yilmaz."

Miles chose that exact moment to holler at us, "We've got it! Need those magic hands of yours, Mahia dear."

As Cain and I stood, I reached out to stop him. "Don't say anything yet. Let's see how this plays out."

<Are you sure?>

<Yes.>

23

The Ray of Confluence

Miles's minions had removed the bones to reveal the largest glyph yet—a Ray of Confluence.

"Well, there's no time like now," I said. "Right?"

"Perhaps if we hold hands, I'll be able to go through with you," Cain said.

I threw him a look of gratitude and disbelief. "Really? You think it could work like that?"

He shrugged. "Worth a try."

"One way to find out," Miles said with an impatient little wave of his hands.

Cracking my neck like I was about to go a round with a suped-up jump fighter, I reached out and touched the glyph. The soft blue light flowed out from my hand and filled the recessed carvings of the pattern. A nervous giggle escaped me, and I withdrew my hand.

"Sorry, I'm not sure where that came from. All right, here I—"

"Sir!" One of the men rushed up to Miles. "We've got a breach at Checkpoint B. Incoming enemy combatants from the east."

"Seal it up, and tell the teams to pull back and meet up at Checkpoint C. After the ten-minute mark, seal it up too. If anyone isn't back to that checkpoint within the next ten minutes, it's game over for them. You can remind them I'm very generous with reimbursing their families."

The man didn't even blink an eye but saluted and left, yelling orders into his comm.

Miles whipped around to me. "Whatever you're going to do, we've just run out of time. If they're coming from the east, then I'm betting Yilmaz was working much faster than I anticipated. Or for longer than I realized." He frowned. "What are you still doing here? Go!"

He didn't leave me any choice. I turned to look at Cain, but Miles shoved me toward the glyph, and before I knew it, my body moved through the rock and into the realm of darkness. *Great. Not again.*

<Cain, can you hear me?>

I sensed our connection, and I thought I heard something whisper through my head, but if he was trying to respond, I couldn't understand him.

<I can't hear you, but if you can hear me, I'm fine for right now. Everything is really dark, wherever I am. Going to take a few steps forward and see what happens. Wishing myself luck.>

I slid one foot forward, wanting to test and make sure I was still going to be on solid ground. The sensory enhancements with the suit were amazing, and I really wished the tech hadn't been so good. As my foot moved, I felt a slight resistance. The floor was solid underneath me, but I was moving through a layer of something—*sticky? No, that's not right.* I slid my other foot forward. *Soft and warm.*

ELIZABETH KNOLLSTON 173

"Hello?" I called out softly, which was a horror story no-no, but I couldn't help myself. "Any… thing out there? I come in peace, I swear." My voice echoed in the darkness, coming back to me distorted.

I shivered and slid forward again. That time, I felt the resistance up along my calf, and as I moved forward once more, I realized whatever coated the ground was climbing. On me.

I backed up as quickly as I could and hit a wall. I turned away and slapped my hands against the rock in the vain hope I could go back. But whatever had allowed me to enter wasn't going to let me out.

I pounded on the wall and yelled, "Cain! Miles! Can you hear me? I'm trapped in here and need—"

The warmth traveled up my legs, spread across my torso, and crawled up my neck. When it reached my face, it paused, and I could feel tendrils of it exploring, trying to find an opening. *Ha, not this time.* The warmth receded and wrapped around my neck and spread down across my back. *Shit.*

Not just some low-level slime or flesh-eating bacteria on a monstrous scale, it was sentient and clever. It was ripping open my suit. I jumped and squirmed, trying to scrape it off, but I could feel it clinging to my skin as it tore open the thin undersuit. Pain bloomed along my spine, starting at the base of my back and rising to my neck. I could do nothing to stop it, and as it ripped through my flesh, I knew I was going to die.

In fairness, I'd already been dead once and had come back to life. *But who in the worlds is lucky enough to have that happen twice? I am, apparently.*

When my awareness returned, I swear I could feel it crawling around *inside* me. After a brief flutter of panic, I realized something else. I could see. Something had turned on the lights. But as I started to look around, to figure out what in Jupiter was going on, I was fairly confident that I wasn't in any actual danger.

I was standing on the edge of an enormous cavern, probably like the others we'd found. But I'd also guessed the others were going to be empty, which would explain why this one had been walled up and protected. Sitting in the middle were three gigantic orbs of metal. My best guess was that they were constructed from the same metallic material as the ship on Dar.

I looked down and, all things considered, was pleased to see a shifting mass of black sand full of twinkling blue lights. That might sound a little strange, my being comforted by that sight, but at least it was something familiar, something I'd already interacted with—the Third.

Is this your natural form? I knelt and moved a hand through the sand. It curled around my fingers as though playing with me. And when I lifted my hand, it followed, imitating my hand's shape. I curled my fingers inward, and it did the same. I made a fist, and it mirrored that too.

Smiling, I stood and stretched. For a brief moment, the Third tried to follow suit but quit and melted back down with the rest of its brethren. Gingerly touching the back of my neck, I could feel the Third running along my spinal column. Its texture wasn't grainy but smooth, as though it'd hardened itself. When I turned around, I caught sight of a few strands of the Third trailing off me into the bulk on the ground. *All right, then. So we're connected. What next?* I wasn't anxious or panicked, merely curious.

I decided to turn my attention to the three orbs. Walking up to them, I could see where they'd been carved with hundreds of glyphs. *Carved or actually made by whatever this is? Could this be the Path Maker? And Pops's elusive machine? But what is that, exactly?*

Deciding the risk was well worth it, I reached out and touched one of the orbs. After a dramatic pause, nothing happened. I was really disappointed. I took a few steps back then slowly walked around all three orbs. The glyphs appeared to be randomly placed, but I couldn't find any discernible pattern that repeated on all three orbs. *Were they three separate machines? Entities? Or one all together but maybe broken into three parts? Were they what was fabricated or what did the fabricating?*

Just for kicks, I tried to push at one but couldn't even budge it. They were massive and solid.

I noted that the Third drifted around them, touching the bases of all of the orbs, and even seemed to coat the entire floor of the chamber. *So that connection doesn't need to be restored. What else had the Two talked about? Oh, right. Something about feeding the One. Great.*

Besides the Third and the orbs, I didn't see anything else in the chamber that appeared to be of use, certainly nothing that implied food or feeding, assuming my assumptions were correct. *Man, that doesn't sound good at all.* I decided a quick jog around the cavern was in order and confirmed my suspicions—nothing.

"Look, we've got to get one thing straight. I'm not food."

A brilliant light flashed at the end of the cavern where I'd come through the wall, and for a moment, I thought the Third had either answered me in some fashion or the Two had transported into the cavern. I was half-right. Someone had transported into the cavern, but it wasn't help.

It was Lucas.

24

Sibling Rivalry

A visibly deformed Lucas—who should've been spending a few more weeks, or even months, in a medical bay—gestured at his own face. "Look familiar?"

I blanched because it did. It was exactly how Lucas had looked during his recovery from when we'd been kids.

"But I shot you."

"That you did, but with the right number of credits, you can get almost any kind of bioupgrade your heart desires. You did some damage—I'll give you points there—but nothing that won't heal with time."

Whatever emotions were trying to pop up, I stomped on them, hard. "How in the hell did you get in here? I thought this is why you needed me?"

Lucas slowly moved toward me and winked. "I did. And you've done beautifully. Minus the whole shooting me, of course. Didn't know whether you had that in you, though."

"But *how*?"

He reached into one of his pockets and brought out his pendant. "Just a little lie here and there, that's all. You're still so gullible. The pendant I'm holding is Pops's. The one you've got is a fabrication designed to suit my needs—a backup option, if you will—in case you decided not to cooperate."

I ripped open my suit—it was torn up by the Third anyway—yanked the necklace off my neck, and chucked it at him. "You played dirty. I should've guessed."

"Yup. Took a page out of our old pops's playbook, tracking you." He bent down to fish it out of the shifting sands of the Third. "But I did have to make adjustments. I knew getting in here was a trick I couldn't accomplish without you. This nifty little piece of tech did several things for me. First, it took some biosamples. Didn't feel a thing, did you?" He grinned. "That's Shelia's bit of expertise. Then we added in some Glipglow tech—have you seen the nails on some of those monstrosities? It's amazing they could figure out how to miniaturize so much tech and cram it into a small space. But with the samples it took and the reports it sent as you moved through the wall… Well, presto chango, here I am."

"A double setup—pretty damn sneaky of you. But I should've realized," I said with a disgusted shake of my head. "You were always so good at getting what you wanted."

"Thanks, sis. Nice of you to say. You know," he said and took a few steps forward while I backed up, "whatever happened down here to you, it was exactly what everyone had been trying to accomplish for generations."

"And what's that?" I spat.

Lucas smiled and gestured toward the orbs. "Getting these beauties to work."

"What would you know of it?"

"A great deal more than you, it appears. I half worried you might have turned them on before I could get here. But thanks to Yilmaz and her hard-work ethic, her forces provided the distraction I needed to transport once into the tunnels, establish the new set of coordinates, and transport again, in here with you. Looks like I'm just in the nick of time."

"I don't think so," I growled. "You know I won't help you."

"Doesn't look like you have a choice." Lucas pointed at the Third. "It's already connecting you."

"So?" I shrugged. "Nothing has happened because of it."

"Perhaps."

Lucas walked up to the orb in the middle and gave it a hearty slap. "Maybe you can finally answer a question that's been dogging me for years. Why did Pops spare you? If he had the answer with you, why not turn in all that information? He would have been crowned a hero. Instead, he dithered around and wasted years of everyone's time. Not to mention what he put me through in order to try to replicate what happened to you."

"Spare me? If you've listened to his journals, then you know the answer. All he wanted was for me to have a normal life."

Lucas laughed and turned toward me. "Normal life?

That old fool. We weren't created for a normal life. We were meant for so much more. You're no help. I'm guessing he just knew how weak you were and that if he reported what had happened, you'd end up embarrassing him and our family."

"Believe whatever you want," I muttered.

"Okay. Here's another one for you, then," Lucas said. "Why did this"—he gestured at the ground—"choose you? I was there too. It could have taken me and not you. So what's the difference?"

"I'm just better looking. Plus, I don't have a black heart," I answered. But I honestly had no idea. *Was it just the luck of the draw? We were siblings, after all. What did I have that Lucas didn't?*

He pursed his lips and turned his attention back to the orbs.

"All right. Now, it's your turn," I said. "If you think I'm the weak one, then why wasn't Pops able to replicate what happened to me with you? I would think that would make you the weak link in the chain."

I thought my question would've provoked him a little. He only laughed, but it didn't reach his eyes. *Good. Two can play this game.*

"How long did he work with you before he knew that you were a dud? Was that why you left? Because you knew you couldn't live up to his expectations? Or were you jealous that Pops loved me more and spared me and not you?"

That hit a tender spot. Lucas turned and lunged for me. I really didn't know what pushing him over the edge was going to accomplish—I just couldn't stand his smug expression. If I'd been thinking clearly, I wouldn't have egged him on, because when it came down to a fight, I wasn't sure I could win. But I needn't have worried. The Third sprang to life and wrapped itself around Lucas, preventing him from moving toward me. He was like a bug caught in a spider's web.

Thanks. But now what? I wasn't any closer to knowing what I was supposed to do, and I certainly wasn't keen on trying to figure it out and give Lucas more fuel for the fire, even if the Third was holding him for the moment.

So I decided to gather a bit more information. "Tell me what you think these are. Fill me in on all that great brainwashing I missed out on."

Lucas struggled against his bonds, but the Third didn't give. In fact, I do believe it got a mite tighter. *Good for it.*

He only glared at me.

"Come on, little brother. If you want me to turn it on, I've got to have some directions, here," I taunted.

I watched as he tried to free one hand then the other. Then I realized in horror that his struggles were ripping off not only his dermal patches but also the newly formed flesh beneath them.

"Stop," I said, moving as close as I dared. "You're only going to hurt yourself even worse. Is that what you want? You'll die here and end up—"

Lucas's irritation turned to that nauseatingly bright smile of someone who'd hit the jackpot. "That's it, isn't it?" he said. "My memories aren't the best from that day. I remember what you did, pushing me down and leaving me. But there's an image stuck in there I haven't been able to shake. You turned around but tripped. Knocked your head or something."

"No," I said. "You're wrong."

But my brother was clever, just like Pops had encouraged us to be. He was putting the last of his pieces of the puzzle together.

"You died, didn't you? And somehow, that was how the connection was formed. It wasn't random chance that it chose you and not me. You simply died before I could've. And who's to say the same won't happen again?" Lucas raged against the Third, which only made it wind its way around even him even more tightly, like an Old Earth boa constrictor—the Lunar Zoo really worked hard at replicating Old Earth animals—suffocating its prey. That only emboldened Lucas even more. At some point, I couldn't stomach it anymore and turned away. Then I heard Lucas gasp, and everything went silent.

Cautiously, I turned back around. The Third was still wrapped around him, keeping him upright. But Lucas was dead. *Don't heal him,* I silently pleaded over and over. *He's not here to help you. Don't heal him. Just let him die.*

With a level of care I couldn't fathom or understand, the Third gently tilted my brother's body to one side and laid him down on the ground. As it unwound, I moved to kneel next to Lucas.

"Why'd you have to turn out to be a damn fool?" I whispered. I reached out to gently close his eyes and couldn't stop the tears from slipping down my cheeks and falling softly into the Third around my feet. I cried for some time until I felt something stirring around me. I stood and wiped away my tears, realizing the Third was moving away from Lucas and from me.

What's going on? I asked but didn't really expect to receive an answer. The Third continued to move, its twinkling blue lights being continually buried as it rolled itself away. As the Third cleared, I noticed a deep groove in the floor on the other side of Lucas, which eventually hit a deeply recessed area of the floor. *How in the world didn't I trip and hurt myself? Thanks to the Third, I guess.*

Not until about half the area was cleared, as the Third moved to hug the walls of the cavern, did I realize what I was seeing. It was the Ray of Confluence but with one added detail. In the center of the glyph was another, much smaller, circular area. I started to move toward it, curious, but the Third, still attached to my spinal column, snapped me backward.

"Wait, what?"

Though I fought against its pull, the Third won out, moving back to join itself against the cavern's walls.

Once the floor was clear of the Third, it lit up the surrounding walls with its blue light, to the point of almost blinding me. But with the harsh blue light illuminating the room, I realized something else. Lucas was sitting up, and a tendril of the Third was coming out from the opposite wall, attached to his back.

"No!" I shouted. "You don't know what you're doing. He'll destroy you if he gets the chance or enslave you, like what happened on Dar."

Lucas was my nightmare come to life. The Third had done a hasty job of healing him or was still in the process—I didn't know which. But half the flesh was gone from his face, revealing the muscles and some bone underneath. His head turned to look at me, but all I saw were two shining orbs of blue light looking back at me. Then he blinked, and the light was gone.

"Never fear, sis, your brother's here." His raspy voice echoed around the room.

He stood and calmly walked backward to a spot opposite me on the wall.

"After all these years, I never dreamed I'd actually get the chance to be the one. I'd only hoped to be here in order to see you make it happen and claim it for my own."

"See what happen?" I whispered.

"Why, the birth of a new age, a new era, where humanity will rule the stars—"

A terrible grinding noise drowned out the last of his words as the three orbs began to move, slowly rolling into place along the Ray of Confluence. Whatever it was that had driven so many to the brink of madness had begun.

25

Cracking the Egg

The orbs slowly rolled, grinding against the floor, then trembled as each settled into place along the Ray of Confluence. Once the last orb slid into its area along the Ray, the Third drifted back toward the orbs, settling into place along the three connecting lines. As it filled those deep grooves, it pulsed with its soft blue light, and each pulse sent a bolt of electricity through my body. I heard the words of the Two echo in my head, and I struggled against the Third. I understood I'd made a pledge to help it, but not like that. Though I tried, I couldn't break free. Together, Lucas and I were dragged across the cavern. The images of all the bodies the Darquets had buried for food for the Third sprang to mind. *Ironic how these things always seem to come full circle.*

Lucas and I were food for the One, and the Third was the conduit.

I continued to fight as long as I could. But with each pulse of light, my energy was dropping drastically. Lucas wasn't struggling at all and had a strange look of pleasure on his mutilated face. *Fanatic.* By the time we were at the edge of the circle in the middle of the Ray, I couldn't physically fight any more. I was too tired. *Guess I'll be going down in history—for what, exactly? Still don't know. But I guess I'll be following in my pops's footsteps after all.*

With an eerie bit of tenderness, the Third lifted us up and placed us within the circle. It was a tight fit and a tad bit uncomfortable.

"I gather this little show was designed for only one?" I said.

Lucas didn't respond, his focus solely on the orbs.

Great. The Third was saturated with light, and the blue glow was flowing to the orbs, filling the multitude of glyphs one by one. It was actually quite beautiful to watch, and I would've enjoyed witnessing this new wonder if it wasn't literally sucking the life out of me.

"Lucas," I said, trying to turn my head to look at him. When he didn't respond, I tried again. "Lucas."

"Hmm?" he responded in a dreamy voice.

"Snap out of it. What's going on? Can you tell me that much, at least?"

He looked longingly at the orb in front of us and sighed. "What we've been waiting for."

"And what exactly is that?"

"Have you ever wondered what's beyond our galaxy?"

I really hadn't, to be honest, and didn't feel like existential questions were important right then. "More of the same? Potential life on distant worlds? Endless combinations of variety?"

He shook his head. "Such a sad, dim outlook. What happened to the wide-eyed wonder of your youth? Continually craving the unknown?"

"I think that took a slightly different turn after our lives were upended," I replied, feeling that stupid need to try to get a rise out of him, wanting to force him to see how wrong he'd been about everything, but I was so tired. My thoughts were slowly drifting toward fuzzy land.

"Maybe if you'd been a better student when it came to our studies about myths and the varied religious outlooks across the known worlds, then you'd realize."

I yawned. "What are you getting at?"

"It's no matter now," Lucas said, unable to stop his own yawn. "What has been hidden has been found. My eyes have been opened, and I watch and wait for the glory to shine upon us."

Lucas closed his eyes, and his head rolled to one side.

"Lucas? Lucas!" I said, but I was feeling so tired, so weak. All I wanted to do was close my eyes and go to sleep. *No. Not yet. Stay awake!* a small voice inside of my head screamed at me. *Fight! Stay awake.*

<Cain? Is that you? I'm sorry we didn't have a longer time to be together.>

But Cain wasn't the one that answered, just the small voice inside me that was still trying to fight. *You ninny. Keep it together.*

My eyes snapped opened, then I yawned again. I did try. I blinked hard a couple of times then opened my eyes as wide as I could make them. All the glyphs on the orbs had been filled with light, and as my eyelids drooped once more, I thought perhaps my vision was beginning to go, because the glyphs appeared to be changing shape. *That can't be. No, wait. Yes, it can. Wasn't that something that happened on Dar? Was that Dar?*

I tried to remember, but even my thoughts were getting sleepy. Something had changed shape—I just couldn't remember exactly what. But it wasn't just the glyphs that were changing. The orbs were vibrating violently until a burst of light shot up out of them into the recessed depths of the cavern.

The shock of the light gave me a fleeting burst of energy as I craned my neck back to trace its path up to the ceiling. It was beautiful. Warmth flooded my body, and my head dropped back down. The light of each orb was expanding, as if something was taking a knife and slowly cutting each orb open. Even though my burst of energy was rapidly dying, I tried to stay focused. *Is each orb a machine, what Pops and so many others had been looking for? What do they do? What's inside them?*

As my questions drifted off into nonsensical absurdities, a violent blast of air and debris crushed me against the edge of the recessed circle the Third had placed me in. My ears rang from the explosion, and as though I was underwater, I could hear muffled shouts and what sounded like weapon fire.

Going down in a blaze of glory, I thought as my eyes drifted shut.

<*Mahia! Wake up!*> The words rang through my head, followed by a not-so-gentle shake.

"I want it shut down. Get them disconnected now!" a woman shouted. "If you don't move, I'll shoot you myself!"

"Is she alive?" someone asked. I didn't recognize the voice.

"Doesn't matter. Orders are orders. Help me with the laser saw. We need to sever their connections. I would cut here"—after a pause, a hand brushed against my neck—"and here. I'll do the spinal. You do the big one."

"Are you saying I don't have a delicate touch?" the first person asked.

"Not now, Reshi. Get the damned saw."

"Yes, sir."

"Get those barricades up. We needed them two minutes ago. Move!" the woman shouted again. "Why aren't they disconnected? They're nearly at twenty-five percent. Get them disconnected!"

I realized that was a voice I knew, and I wished I didn't. The sound of her shouting orders snapped me out of my sleep, and I looked up at the worried face of none other than Commandant Yilmaz. She caught me watching and gave me a curt nod. "Once those connections are cut, I want Lucas Orion secured—bound and gagged, do you understand?" She received a chorus of *yes, sir*s before she strode off, shouting at a new group of people.

I felt and heard a crackle then a pop followed by an intense burst of pain. I arched my back and screamed.

"Stop, you're going to kill her," someone said.

"And if I don't finish, Yilmaz will kill me. There, almost done."

The white-hot pain rushed down my spine and burst through my entire body.

"Hold him back, or else this isn't going to work!"

"If you hurt her... I'll—" a beautiful voice growled. *<Hang in there. They're almost done.>*

I squeezed my eyes shut and tried to breathe through the pain. *<What's going on?>*

<Just breathe, and hold on.>

"There," the voice said triumphantly. "Got 'em. Get those gags on Lucas, quick! And let's get them out of—"

"Back off. We've got her."

I tilted my head back to stare up at Cain. *<Hi.>*

"Hi yourself," he said as he jumped down into the circle—once Lucas had been dragged out—and began to lift me up.

"Wait, I don't think—"

But Cain picked me up, turned, and lifted me up into the waiting arms of Miles.

"What about the Third? It connected itself—"

"Just hold still. That's been taken care of," Cain reassured me.

"Chambers! Get over here!" Miles yelled. "And where are those shields? We need to get shielding up in here."

<What in the worlds is going on?>

"We've found her, and my part of the deal is over. I'm taking her, and we're leaving," Cain growled.

"I think that should be up to—" Miles started but switched gears. "No, Pytha, the shielding. Forget about them!"

"Come on, I need you to get up. We've got to find a way out of here," Cain said as he pulled himself up out of the hole. *<We don't have much time.>*

"What's going on?" I asked, trying to push myself

up, but I was so weak that all I could do was collapse back to the ground.

"You're not going anywhere, and you know it. We're cut off in all directions," Miles snapped. "Those idiots have a scrambler set up. We can't transport out, and we can't call for help."

"You might be, but she's not. We'll find a way out," Cain replied. His eyes were pitch black. "I'm not staying here to be fodder for Yilmaz. Nor is Mahia. We aren't going to be a part of her grand scheme or any other little science experiment she might cook up. She's got Lucas for that now."

"Of course not," Miles said. "I won't allow it—you know that."

Cain was ready to strike. "Just like you made the agreement with her? What else did you give up in order for her to help us? What did you promise?"

"Stop, both of you," I tried to say, but it came out as a whisper, and neither of those hotheads heard me, or at least they pretended they didn't.

Cain made the first move, but Miles was ready. Each one landed a few blows on the other, and I struggled to push myself up. Out of sheer will—or anger, because they were really getting on my nerves—I stood.

"Knock it off, you two. What the hell is going on?" I swayed as the room spun. *Oh, goodie. I'm going to fall.* But I toppled to one side into a pair of waiting arms. I looked up at Chambers.

"Grow up, the both of you!" he bellowed while carefully helping me hobble to one side of the cavern. "You need to stay still for a bit. Let me check you over." He looked up at Miles and Cain, who'd stopped moving. "Miles, go grab my med kit. And Cain, help me with her."

Both men looked ashamed, as they should've been. Cain took over for Chambers.

"Tell me what's going on," I said. *<Now.>*

"Have Chambers check you over," Cain said as he helped me down so that I could lean against the wall. He gently brushed my loose hair away from my face. *<We've got to find a way out of here. Do you know any other ways in or out?>*

I coughed but shook my head. *<I didn't have that much time. Lucas showed up and—>*

Miles was back, and Chambers took the med kit and knelt next to me. He checked my vitals and pulled out an edible water bottle. He unscrewed the top and dropped in a couple of different pills, which bubbled and fizzed. "Drink this, and try to stay quiet for the next ten to fifteen minutes. It's not great, but the stims will help get you back on your feet."

I pushed the bottle away. "Sorry, doc. No stims for me, thanks."

He huffed and looked up at Cain, who stared back at Chambers. With another huff, he said, "Fine." He dug through his medical pack and ended up giving me a couple of different shots. He mumbled what they were for, but as long as they weren't stims, I didn't care. He handed me another edible bottle, and I eyed it with suspicion.

"Not laced with anything, but you're severely dehydrated. Drink it, then eat it. Doctor's orders. Now, if you'll excuse me…" Chambers gave me a tight smile, stood, and left.

As I lifted the bottle to my mouth, the floor shook, and I heard a renewed volley of weapons fire and shouting.

Cain leaned over me and growled, "Miles, if you don't help us leave, I'm going to—"

Miles looked exhausted, and all his fight appeared to be gone. "Look, shielding should be up in… one minute and thirty seconds. Then we've got approximately thirty minutes until Lio is in orbit. And I'm counting on him to get us out of this mess."

"And by then, Yilmaz could overrun us. I'm not going back," Cain said.

Miles looked annoyed. "I don't know how many times I've got to tell you, but I won't let that happen."

"Like I'd believe in your promises," Cain snapped.

The water and whatever else Chambers had given me were doing the trick. I took another long drink then said. "Boys, I'm severely lacking information here and am tired of not following your bickering."

"You've been in here for a little over twenty-three hours," Cain said.

I almost choked on my water. "Excuse me? I'm getting really tired of this missing-time crap. Are you sure?"

Cain looked at me, his eyes mostly black with flecks of amber. "Yes."

"And in that time, you decided to play nice with Yilmaz? Did I wake up in an alternate reality or something?"

"Shields are up, sir," someone called over to Miles.

He visibly relaxed. "We'll explain what happened on our end if you can explain what happened here." Then Miles turned and pointed at the orbs.

At least I hadn't imagined everything. All three of the little orbs were still there and slowly splitting open.

26

Unholy Alliances

I shrugged but immediately regretted the gesture because it hurt, and I took another drink. "I guess I fed the One."

"That's not an answer," Cain said.

"I know." I sighed. "But I really don't know exactly what happened." I gave them the details, which made them both seem disappointed. "I wish I understood, but I don't." *I'm so tired of these headaches.* I set the bottle down and rubbed my temples, trying to keep up with what was going on.

"Same thing with Yilmaz except I think she's lying to us," Miles muttered.

"How astute of you," Cain muttered.

"You really need to fill me in," I said and cringed at another round of weapon fire.

"Your brother's buddies decided they didn't like us anymore," Miles quipped. "Go figure."

I rolled my eyes and looked at Cain.

"We were ambushed right before you went through the wall," Cain added.

"'Got pushed' is more like it."

Miles had the good graces to blush. "Yes, well. Time was of the essence." He coughed. "Turns out Lucas and his minions had been fighting Yilmaz, who'd been trying to push through to our location. But they were pinned down and sorely outnumbered since they'd cut her off from the *Justus*. So I negotiated a temporary alliance, which I can bet you won't hold when we're finished. So be on guard."

"Good enough," I said and tried to stand.

"No. Not good enough," Cain said. "I didn't make any agreements with Yilmaz, and I've helped you hold this area long enough to get to Mahia. And now we're leaving."

"No, we're not," I said, making Cain actually looked startled. *<I've started something, and I need to see it through.>*

<You don't owe anyone a thing. We know what your father was after. We've got the answers. Now, we need to leave before it's too late. Let the rest of them fight it out.>

"Miles," I whispered.

He understood. He left, barking more orders.

"Cain, I don't like Yilmaz any more than you. And I didn't go through what you did, so I can't understand the depths of your hatred right now." I was feeling a lot more than hatred through our connection—Cain was afraid. "But remember what you told me about fear?" I hated asking the question, the implication behind it. I appreciated Cain's support and nudging me in the right direction, but right then, I needed to do the same for him.

"And do you remember what else I told you?" Cain

asked, pulling back. "That I would follow you no matter what you decided?"

A wave of guilt rushed over me because I did remember. My eyes moved to the orbs, merrily doing their thing despite the chaos and bloodshed around them. Another wave of guilt washed over me, and I felt drawn toward them. I'd started something that needed to be finished. And I needed to understand why Lucas had been willing to die to take a chance to be a part of whatever this was. If he'd wanted it, then I definitely didn't. And I wasn't liking the implications that my helping the Third played right into everyone's hands.

But Cain was my heart's blood, who'd stood by me through my crazy journey. *If I walk away from what he needs, then how am I any different from Pops, who walked away from me? He'd wanted me to be safe, to have a normal life, but instead of turning away from the Sun Worshipers and giving it all up, he tried to have the best of both worlds, protecting me but still pushing ahead with them. And in the end, his actions still sacrificed me anyway.*

I looked back at Cain, who'd hung his head. I grabbed his hands and pulled him toward me. "Okay," I whispered. "We'll find a way out of here—in order to avoid Yilmaz double-crossing us. But if we can get out, then we can help Miles and his team get out too. Let Yilmaz deal with Lucas's gang."

I sensed he wanted to protest, but he kept it to himself. He helped me stand, and we made our way over to Miles, who was talking with Ochoa. A wave of relief flooded me as I saw her standing and listening to him. Even though I didn't really know her, I was irrationally happy to see her.

She gave me a tight smile when she looked up. "Patched me up. It'll hold for what's to come. Good to see you're still kicking."

"It's good to see you too," I said. "What do you think is coming? More of Lucas's followers?"

"Yes. More than we'd realized. I don't know what kind of tech they've gotten their hands on, but they were total ghosts to all our scans. If I had my guess, I'd say the entire group of Sun Worshipers have converged on Epo-5."

<All the more reason to seek safety,> Cain silently commented.

"And you think you'll be able to beat them back?" I asked.

Ochoa gave me a shrewd look. "Yes, I think we will. With what's left of Yilmaz's crew plus what Miles brought. And Lio is inbound. We just need to hold this position until he arrives and can punch through the scramblers to get us out of here."

I gave a small nod and looked around at everyone holding our position, putting their lives on the line, then my gaze swung to Miles.

"Can I talk with Miles?" I asked.

Ochoa nodded and moved a discreet distance off to one side.

Miles took one look at me then at Cain. "So, you've agreed with him, then, have you?"

"How do you do that?"

"Years of reading the political landscape, I suppose."

"Look, Cain's right. Yilmaz will only turn against us. Besides, why are you helping her? You know we can't trust her. And we can't risk being arrested by the IGJ when all of this is over here. I've got a feeling this isn't the last of it." I hadn't realized I had that feeling until the words rolled off my tongue.

Miles's raised an eyebrow. "Really? You don't think the convention of the Sun Worshipers spells out the final act to this whole deal? We've got what they want, what they've been searching for, right?"

"Yes," I said, eyeing the orbs and realizing what was bothering me. "But where are the Two? They told me they'd come when the Ray of Ascension had been revealed. So"—I waved a hand around—"if this is it, then where are they? There's more to this, and getting blown up or arrested by Yilmaz isn't going to do any of us any good. Look, we all need a way out of here, right? Cain and I will find it, then we'll come back and help you and your team get out. You'll have to do something to distract Yilmaz, but maybe we can find a way out and get out of range of the scramblers—beam up, or whatever, and regroup."

"Why, Mahia Orion, I do believe you've grown sweet on me," Miles teased. "But you're right. You're the only one who could scout a way out. Do what you need to, and I'll work on how to deal with Yilmaz." He motioned at Ochoa. "Grab some gear. You're going with these two knuckleheads."

"Sir," Ochoa nodded.

"Miles, we don't need a babysitter," Cain growled.

"That isn't why I'm sending her. I trust Mahia's

instincts. If something doesn't feel right, then she needs to figure it out. And if we lose, I don't want her to get captured by the Sun Worshipers or Yilmaz. Despite what you two might think, I don't trust her either. She's merely a tool I can use at the moment. Ochoa will be a good match for you, Cain. We know that already. And another pair of eyes doesn't hurt. Plus, she can get me tactical intel. I'd go with you, but someone has to keep Yilmaz in line."

I gave Miles a hug. "Thank you," I whispered.

"Look after him," Miles said under his breath. He pulled back and extended a hand to Cain. "I know we're not best friends or even pen pals. But I promise you, just as I would've made a promise to your sister, that I will do everything in my power to keep Yilmaz away from you two."

Though I wasn't sure Cain was going to accept, he did. "I will hold you to it."

Ochoa had returned and handed Cain a pack. "Where's mine?" She patted the straps over her shoulder. "We've got enough for all of us. Right now, let's keep you free to do what you do best."

I didn't like the idea of not pulling my weight, but I wasn't going to argue. Though Chambers's drugs had helped, I wasn't feeling one hundred percent myself yet. "All right, let's find a way out of here."

We slowly crept into the shadows of the cavern. "I did a quick tour of the area when I first came in here, but I didn't see anything right away. We need to look for anything that might be a glyph. That'll be our ticket out of here."

Cain nodded, and we all searched the walls as surreptitiously as we could. I couldn't focus, even though I tried. *Whether we stay and fight won't make a difference. Miles knows what he's doing, and he brought a whole team of people with him. They can defeat Lucas's horde. And Cain is right. We can't trust Yilmaz. We find a way out of here, and once we're safe, I can return to figuring out what's going on.*

My conflicting emotions were strange. Just a few months before, I'd been on my own, keeping my head and just moving through life. Now, I wasn't alone, and I was conflicted over this decision. Cain came first. He had to. But Miles—as slippery as he was—had continued to be there for us even if he'd been playing different angles at times. He could've cut his losses after Dar and never returned, yet he'd committed himself and his resources to help. *No. He knew what he was doing. And he was the one who made the agreement with Yilmaz.*

I ran my hands along the wall and tried to make sense of any gouges here or there. The fighting had intensified, and my chest was tight. *What if we don't win? What if the barricades don't hold? What then?*

<*I think I've found something.*>

I hurried over to Cain and examined the section of wall he was pointing at. We were almost exactly opposite where'd I'd entered, and I'd missed it my first time around. But it was there—the glyph the Two had reacted so poorly to. *Would it act like the Ray of Confluence? What does it signify?* But I didn't have time to think like a xenologist or be analytical like Pops would've been. Instead, I raised my hand and let it hover over the glyph.

"What makes you think this will work?" Ochoa asked.

"A hunch," I said. I focused on the glyph and the memory of the sensation of the Third digging its way into my spinal column. Warmth spread across my back, flowed down my arms, and through my hand. I was glowing. I pressed my hand against the glyph, and it melted into the wall. With a confident smile, which Cain didn't share, I reached out to take his hand. "Shall we?"

<Are you...>

I understood. Not a lot of words could've expressed the complex emotions working through both of us. *<I'm okay. And I'm sure.>* I tilted his hand to show him, how tendrils of the Third were extending from my hand to wrap around his.

"Now, Ochoa, grab Cain's other hand." Once she did and the Third had spread to connect the three of us together, I pushed us through the wall. As I emerged into another dark expanse, my confidence waned, and I was afraid I would turn around to see Cain or Ochoa stuck in the wall. But they both squeezed my hands in reassurance, and a huge sigh of relief escaped my lips.

"Would have been helpful to have known before that it worked that way," Cain muttered.

"It wouldn't have. What happened has changed me," I said.

But that conversation was put on hold as Cain and Ochoa turned up the lights on their suits and illuminated the darkness.

We'd stepped directly into hell.

27

A Smidge of Understanding

Pops had been looking for mass graves. He just hadn't been looking in the right place. Not that I could blame him—no alien entity had decided to be friends with him then go and change his genetic makeup to suit its needs.

Ochoa raised her weapon, and Cain took a step forward and moved in front of me. But I gently pushed him to the side and took stock of where we were.

Thick, hard knots of what had once been the Third were suspended throughout the cavern. This one didn't have the feel of being as large as the one with the orbs, but it was still sizable. Tangled within the dark and lifeless strands of the Third were skeletons—hundreds upon hundreds of skeletons. They reminded me of the Sici—squat, wide trunks with thick ribs, legs bent back at an angle, and skulls with horns protruding up from the center. But from what I remembered of Pops's discussion of the neighboring Sici, these skeletons appeared to have four arms rather than two. And if a proper excavation was done of the bone tunnel, I was quite sure researchers would discover the same skeletal remains there that we were seeing in this cavern.

I stepped forward and slowly approached the nearest skeleton.

"Don't," Cain said.

"Everything is dead here. Even the Third," I reassured him.

Ochoa tried to back him up. "That might be true, but we don't know—"

Turning to look at them both, I lifted my hand and found I was still glowing with the soft blue light. "I'm sure."

I turned back to the closest skeleton and reached out to gently trace the contours of the skull. It had a thick mandible with sharp canines. *Carnivore? Or omnivore?* My fingers moved upward and along the cracked edges of the frontal bone, below the curved horn. Protruding from the skull was a thin strand of the Third, which extended outward a way and tapered off to a sharp point. As I moved slowly through the macabre scene, I realized the majority of the skeletons had been pierced by the Third. Not all of them were through the skull—some had strands of the Third going through their ribs, and a few had it woven through their spinal columns.

Something was oddly familiar about the whole scene. *Is it because I'm carrying the Third within me? I'm sensing a memory or recognition?* I didn't think so. I ducked underneath a pair of skeletons, their arms reaching out to each other, with the Third wrapped around each arm bone. *Had the Third posed them like that, or had they been reaching for each other?* For an instant, I pictured Cain and myself suspended there instead of the skeletons.

<I'm right here.>

I looked over at him for reassurance.

"Mahia? What do you want to do? Look for an exit or go back?" Ochoa asked.

"You guys look for an exit. I need to explore a bit."

Despite all her training, she seemed a little spooked by the sight, but I didn't blame her. This was the stuff nightmares were made of. Ochoa exchanged a few words with Cain then moved off to scout the perimeter of the cavern.

"What are we looking for?" Cain asked quietly. "Another set of glyphs?"

"I'm not sure. But something," I said. We ducked and moved carefully through the graveyard, not wanting to disturb any of it. As we made our way to the center, I realized why it all felt familiar.

"Triton," I breathed.

"What?" Cain asked.

I pointed at the skeleton in the middle of the area. It was raised off the ground, several strands of the Third protruding from it and one thick cord of the Third shooting up out of the skull all the way to the ceiling.

"This reminds me of Triton, Mrs. Gol's son on the *Rapscallion*. He had been suspended in some kind of stasis chamber—I'm assuming—and had lots of tubes coming out of his body." I turned to look at Cain. "They must have found sites similar to this one, taken samples of the Third, and tried to replicate what it was trying to do. But they kept getting it wrong, just like whatever happened here went wrong. And down the line, they must've figured out that there needed to be some kind of genetic match, something the Third was looking for in order for complete"—I used air quotes here—"union."

"I think you need to come see this," Ochoa called out.

I threw Cain a hasty look, then we carefully made our way over to where her light illuminated something unexpected.

"A local inhabitant?" she asked.

Standing at least a head taller than Cain was a solidified shell of a humanoid figure, with one arm stretched out, pointing at something in the distance.

"No, I don't think so," I replied, slowly working my way around it. "It's too tall and lacks some of the features we're seeing in the skeletons. Unless there were more than one species that evolved on this world."

"Or visited it, at least," Cain added.

"Possible," I murmured.

I took a step closer and gently reached out to the side of the figure, and a flash of blue light illuminated the spot I'd touched. "Fudge nuggets!" I yelped and jumped back.

"Perhaps we should keep our hands to ourselves," Ochoa said and moved off. "Looks like we might have some potential glyphs up ahead."

Cain walked off to investigate with her then must've realized I hadn't followed, because he stopped and called out, "Mahia?"

But I didn't respond. I was puzzling over the figure and the flash of blue light. The thick, hard exterior looked exactly like the strands of dead Third. *Did it completely engulf someone? Or did it mold itself into this form?* Curious, I turned to face the direction the figure pointed.

I slowly moved in that direction, and as Cain joined me and flashed his light, we discovered a second figure.

This one reminded me of Elea and the other Darquets who'd been forced to serve the Third and the Holy One in the center of the cavern. The figure's frozen body had its arms stretched up above its head, back arched. And extending out of its hands were tendrils of the Third. Cain's light flashed over those tendrils and, tracing their path, I was pretty sure they were the source of the web of death in this cavern.

"Mahia. Cain. I need to you to check these glyphs out—might be the ticket out of here," Ochoa called out.

"Cain, go see what she's found," I said absentmindedly.

"No."

I turned to face him, his eyes a deep emerald.

"Go to Ochoa, Cain. I know what I need to do, and I don't want you to get caught up in it."

<No. Where you go. I go. Together.>

I stepped up to him and lay a hand against the thin material of the suit covering his face. "And I appreciate that. But this is something I must do. And do alone."

My hand began to glow softly, and the Third traveled down my arm to wrap itself around Cain. He tried to struggle, to protest, but I wasn't going to let him. I pushed him back toward Ochoa, and when she realized what was happening, she leapt forward, but I spun another thin thread of the Third and used it to hold her back as well.

<Stop. This isn't you. Mahia. You need to take control.>

I ignored the voice in my head, and when I was satisfied they wouldn't be able to interfere, I reached out and touched the figure, the Third slowly extending out of my fingers and burrowing into the shell of what once had been its brethren. I closed my eyes and let the vision—or memory—wash over me.

Something was wrong with the sea of light. Its surface was dull and unnaturally still. Even the sand, once a vibrant black, was bleached almost bone white. What I'd come to assume was the Celestial Light—the Two before everything went wrong—stood off to the side, their hands palm down and the ground vibrating beneath their feet. Tendrils of the Third shivered and changed into different glyphs, but I instinctively knew the glyphs were incomplete and jumbled up with other incomplete glyphs. *Fear?*

The beings of light bowed their heads, and up from the ground rose a multitude of orbs. The Third moved to cover the orb, sinking into each delicately carved glyph on its surface, while the beings of light tilted their heads back and stared at the sky. A void was hanging above us, deep and black and full of fury. I raised a hand as the light from the pair grew too bright to watch, and they engulfed the orbs, lifting them high above the ground and toward the void.

Pain trickled down my neck, my spine, my arms, and my legs. It intensified until I felt as if every atom of my being was slowly being ripped apart. Piece by piece, my flesh separated from my muscles, then my bones were ground into fine powder, and when I was no more, I was also swept up into the void.

Inside the void was nothing.

Inside the void was everything.

Inside the void was no time.

Inside the void was all time.

Starlight slowly winked into existence, and piece by piece, I felt my bones form and settle back into shape. My muscles stretched across my skeleton, and my flesh returned, whole and new. But when I lifted my hand to stare at it in wonder, something was wrong. I wasn't complete. We weren't complete. I stretched myself as long and thin as we could be, searching for those who were formed to protect that which I watched over. I was incomplete without that for which we were formed, for what I nurtured, what we would care for.

<*Mahia!*> My eyes snapped open, and the Third pulled away from the figure. I turned and slowly walked back to the other silent figure and stretched my hand toward it, the Third once more pushing through its dead brethren's flesh.

<*No. You are losing yourself. Hold on to who you are. Hold on to me.*>

I heard the voice but ignored it.

I was standing on a world alien to me. Its soft earth was covered in something foreign. But I sensed the orbs, buried deep within the earth, waiting for me to bring them the sustenance they required to grow and mature. They needed me. They needed those who guarded them. I waited for the guardians to bring us the light and the energy we would transfer to the orbs, but they did not come. The orbs cried out to me, and we stretched ourselves as far and wide as I could, trying to absorb the light from a sun that was so distant, so cold to touch.

I stretched out a small tendril, curious but cautious, and touched the thin strands of something that was alive but not alive in the sense I was familiar with. Sunlight bathed my body, and I rejoiced, but it was so far away, too far away without the others to feed me so that I in turn could feed them. The orbs were dying, unable to accept what I offered. Furious and frightened, we explored, and I sensed life deep underground. It was small and fleeting, but I reached out to touch it and discovered we could take from it and restore my strength—not from the light but from the life found crawling beneath the dirt.

Did I always have this ability? Or did the void change us when it formed us in this place?

I sent another tendril deep within the ground and found more life and took it for our own. But a part of me fought against this newfound source of energy. This wasn't what I was created for. I was to take that which was harvested and nurture the Path Makers. My Vow upon the Celestial Plain was to nurture and protect the life yet to come. *But where are the others who had stood with me when the Vow was created?* They had left me here. Abandoned us. Abandoned the life within the orbs.

So I stretched myself down, deep within the dirt, and took all we needed. I gave this newfound source of energy to the orbs, to that which we watched over, but it rejected my gifts, my nurturing.

I blinked and saw the same story play out on a different world. But this time, the Third made contact with the indigenous population. They tried to join but were unable. They tried to communicate but were unable.

Fear drove them deep underground, where they hid, withered, and died.

I blinked and saw the same story play out on a different world. The Third was cautious as it searched for those who made the Vow upon the Celestial Plain. Finding none, they took life only when needed, hiding and waiting in the dark.

I blinked and saw the same story play out on a different world. The Third took the life and fed it to the orbs, but they were discovered and destroyed.

I blinked and saw the same story play out on a different world.

I blinked—

28

Who Am I?

I stumbled forward, inadvertently bumping into the frozen Third. Horrified, I watched as it crumbled into a pile of dust. *I'm sorry. We're so sorry.*

"Mahia!" Cain called out.

My vision blurred, and we saw two living things lashed to the wall. I stretched myself, spinning tendrils of us toward them—hungry, so desperately hungry. I had begun the process of feeding the Path Makers, but something happened and stopped the process. They were the last, and if I didn't finish what I was created to do, then I would fail. We would die.

<This isn't you. Mahia Orion, you are not the Third. You are an individual, a unique human being. You are my heart's blood. Remember who you are.>

I fell to my knees, trying to ignore the flood of images assaulting me. *I was sitting next to an older woman. I was walking down a hallway and bumped into a rather handsome man. I was lying in a corridor, dying and surrounded by the man and Glipglows. I was fearless as I stalked through the halls of a dead ship. I was scared as I faced the woman. I was grinning* *at the man. <This is who you are and so much more. You are smart, annoying, and compassionate. You are fearless and brave.>*

But we were not these things. We were meant to serve, to be the caretakers of the orbs, of the life upon the Celestial Plain. We danced along the shores of the Endless Light and shone bright with the Rays of Contentment. We burrowed into the warm black sand and cradled the orbs, passing on the light from those above to those below.

I'm fascinated with a piece of art someone is showing me. I'm brave as I try to face my demons. I'm curious as I seek answers. I'm fearless as I stand up to those who would hurt the one I love. I'm reckless and frustrating as I risk it all and travel by myself to a place of danger. <Come back to me, my heart's blood. See who you are.>

But we are not these—*No. I'm these things, but you aren't. We aren't the same. Thank you for sharing yourself with me. I think I understand, but I'm not you, and you aren't me.*

We are not these things. *No, you're not. We are different. We are separate.*

I looked up at Cain and tried to smile, but I was so tired. As I tried to stand up, my legs gave out, and I fell back down to my knees, my hands splayed against the cold, hard rock. *<I'm so tired, Cain. I don't know how much more of this I can take.>*

With a roar, Cain broke free of the Third and rushed over to me. "Mahia, my heart's blood. Please," he whispered.

"I think I'm okay. I swear. Just really worn out. I feel like I've traveled halfway across the galaxy in a matter of minutes. Just need a sec to recoup," I said, leaning into him. *Who knows? I think I've might have just really traveled all that way.*

<Why did you do it?>
<Because I had to. I needed to know.>
<And now?>

"Now, I do," I mumbled. "Hang on." I looked over his shoulder at Ochoa and unwound the Third holding her up against the wall. She gave me a troubled look but moved to join us. "Sorry about that. Just didn't want to accidentally dig into the two of you. I wasn't sure it would work—just following a hunch."

"A hunch," she said. "Good or bad?"

"Both, I think. But I know we need to go back. I need to finish what was started. I don't understand half of what I've seen or why it needed someone like me, but those orbs… They're important."

"Are you sure?" Cain asked.

I nodded. "It's not a great option at all, but I can't let anyone else get to those orbs. I'm not sure where it all went wrong, but they're not machines or some kind of great power source. They're…"—I struggled here—"the last of their kind, I think."

"And what, exactly, is that?" Ochoa asked.

"Baby Star Eaters. Or rather, whatever the Two are or were. Beings from the Celestial Plain."

They both stared at me. I wasn't expecting them to be so startled by my pronouncement. *I mean, come on, really? After everything that's happened?* But they hadn't seen what I had.

"Explain to me how that is possible," Ochoa said.

I really considered how to answer her, but in the end, I shrugged. "I don't know. I was given snatches of memories—I think, no, I'm confident—and all I can tell you is that the Third serves as an… umbilical cord of some kind. Where it should be taking from the Two to nourish what's inside the orbs. But something went wrong when they traveled here, and…" I shook my head. "Beyond that, I'm not sure. There are still quite a few holes in what I've been shown."

"Traveled here," Cain said with a concerned look. "Like what we saw on Dar? So the orbs are also some type of ship?"

I scrunched up my face. "Yes? No? Both? They all traveled through something together. Sorry, that's all I understand right now."

"We need more intel," Ochoa muttered.

"I agree, but—" I sensed the Third and its frustration. *It's okay. Hang on. I'm going to help you.* But the frustration remained, and I sensed something else, another presence nestled within the Third.

"What is it?" Cain asked.

"Can you feel that?" I asked. *<Can you feel the Third with me?>*

He briefly closed his eyes, and I sensed his presence rooting around in my head, but when he opened them, his eyes were a bright emerald. "No. Nothing."

"We need to go back," I said again, really meaning it this time. "Something is wrong."

I had no rational explanation for how I knew—I just did. Finding a way out and avoiding being snared by Yilmaz—again—had been important. But leaving wasn't an option right then. I had to go back to the chamber with the orbs.

"Tactically, this isn't a great decision," Ochoa said. "You are important, and if we go back, we could be playing right into several different traps, along with the real chance of not surviving the fire fight out there." She and Cain helped me to my feet as she spoke.

"I know," I replied. "And if you want to—"

"Don't even insult me by finishing that sentence," she said.

"Sorry," I said and blushed.

"Did Lio tell you why I signed on with him?" she asked.

I blushed again. "He shared a little bit with me."

Ochoa grinned. "Then you should know I'm with you. One hundred percent—even if I don't understand what in the hell is going on. But Lio asked me to help you, and so I'm here. For you. At your disposal. And yes, I mean that quite literally. Blame my training on that little flaw." Her words were soothing and unnerving at the same time.

"Thanks. I think."

She laughed and took point as we carefully made our way back to the other side of the cavern.

"Is there anything else you can share with me?" Cain asked. I had an arm slung over his shoulders, and he gripped my torso like I was going to be yanked out of his arms at any moment. Honestly, it felt good.

"Did you see anything that I experienced? We've shared memories before," I said.

"Nothing. It was like a dark wall of the Third between you and me."

"Huh." *Where to start?* "Then I'll tell you—both of you"—Ochoa waved a hand in acknowledgment—"what I can." And in the few short minutes we took to get back to the other side, I filled them in. To say we were all a little more confused than when we'd started would be an understatement.

"Right, so when we go through, Mahia, I need you to let go and step off to the side. Let Cain and me take point. We don't know what we're going to be walking into. Clear?"

"Clear."

I reached out and took their hands with both of mine, the Third winding its way down my arms once more and up theirs. With my body radiating a gentle blue light, I stepped through the wall once more and pulled them along with me.

29

The Sun Worshipers

Yilmaz, in her arrogance—or her soldiers in their igno-
rance—hadn't properly secured Lucas. The Third had
stretched out from his body and wrapped itself around
the men and women guarding him. And judging from
the tangled web of bodies, the energy it'd gotten from
the guards allowed it to explode throughout the room.
Each subsequent person it ensnared allowed it to spread
farther and farther until it had snaked its way around
everyone. By the time we stepped back into the cavern,
no one had been spared.

Cain and Ochoa stepped in front of me, ready to
defend, but I stopped them. "Behind me," I said. I wasn't
sure if the Third that was a part of me would help or
try to rejoin with itself, but I had to take the chance and
see if I could reason with it. *We are not your enemies. But
we are not your food either. I've come to help. If you try to feed the
Path Makers, you will kill them. We can find a different way to
protect them, to nurture them.*

My hands took on a soft blue hue, and I caught sight
of movement off to my right. The Third within the

cavern had sensed our presence, and a thin tendril spun up out of the cocoon it'd made around the nearest body. *Please. Help me so we can finish what you were created to do. You were with me, a part of me. You saw what I saw. This isn't the way. This will kill the Path Makers.*

The Third snaked down my arms and dripped off my fingertips, rapidly building a protective barrier around the three of us. *Thank you.* Lucas's Third probed the barrier, and I could sense its presence pushing back against me. *See what I saw. Take from me, not from Lucas. He isn't here to help you. He's here for his own gain.* I wasn't sure it would understand, but I really hoped so. I could feel its hunger and desperation, the need to perform its duty. But it didn't try to break through the barrier, which was a plus.

"Mahia, we need options," Ochoa said.

"I know. I'm working on it." I took a step forward, the three of us inching closer to the nearest orb as one.

"Miles," Cain said and touched my arm.

I looked over my shoulder, and my chest tightened. Miles was leaning against a wall, half of his body coated in the Third, with thin tendrils reaching up his back and wrapped around his neck. He blinked and looked right at us.

At least he's still alive and aware.

"Hang on, Miles. We're going to figure this out," I said.

He blinked again. I did a quick scan of the room and found Yilmaz not too far away from Lucas. *She must have realized what was happening and rushed over to try to stop it.*

"How do we fix this?" Ochoa asked.

I rubbed my head in frustration. The Third's need to complete its duty was overpowering, clouding my judgment. I wanted to help—I'd promised to help—but not like this. Another way had to exist, a way to fix the symbiotic relationship between the Two and the Third. *The Two—that's it.* "We've got to get the Two. I think they're the only ones who can stop this."

"But how?" Cain asked. "And do you really think they will? Weren't they the ones who set you up for all of this?"

"Yes… no. But not like this. They didn't ask to be cut off from the Third. It was an accident, a mistake. We've got to try."

The idea I was forming wasn't great, not even good. But it was the only idea I could come up with. "I need the two of you to step back. I'll create a shield around you, but I need to have space."

<No.>

<Cain, I can't—>

<No. This time, I won't.>

"Since Cain's not moving, I'm taking it he's refusing? Because that's good. I am too," Ochoa said.

"I don't know what's going to happen, and I—"

"Girl, you've got to learn what it means to have backup. Do your thing. We're here."

<I'm here—with you, no matter what.>

A rush of love and confidence flooded my mind and body. I didn't feel like I deserved it, but I held on to it. I still wanted to fight back and push them away, just like I had in the other chamber. But Cain and Ochoa—smart little buggers—reached out and grabbed my hands, and some of the anxiety in my chest relaxed. I wasn't alone, not this time. *Not ever again.*

"This may hurt a bit," I said.

"I think that's an understatement now," Ochoa said.

"Do whatever you need to," Cain added.

All right. Buckle up, 'cause here we go. I closed my eyes and concentrated. *The Ray of Ascension must be completed, but it can't be done through the flesh and energy you're consuming. Let me guide you. Let me do what you've been hoping for and find a way back to what you were created to do.*

I felt the entire room focus on me, and I opened my eyes and let out a small sigh of relief as my Third responded with a myriad of dancing blue lights. I envisioned in my mind what I wanted to happen.

<Cain, if you can see what I'm thinking, I need you to help me. Picture it with me.>

<I can do that.>

"Ochoa, I know you're not mentally linked in with us, but I want you to focus on this. Picture the Third as a thick trunk of a tree that's stretching up through the chamber to the ceiling. Its thick trunk is pushing up through the rock, finding a way to the light. Can you do that?"

"Yup."

"Good. We need to break through the cavern and get the Two's attention on the surface."

I knew a component was still missing. The Two had seen the Third when it'd protected me from them. So it wasn't just a matter of being physically separated. *Once we reach them, I've got to figure out what they need to join, for the union to be healed.*

The Third responded to us, and it shifted, and even our barrier melted away to join the bulk of the Third as it molded and shaped itself into one thick, winding trunk. Slowly, it climbed, building on top of itself over and over until it reached the ceiling. *Push. You need to push through the rock. Find the cracks and crevices. Move through them and create the space you need.*

"Mahia, I think we've got to speed things up here," Ochoa said.

I broke my concentration for a fraction of a second and glanced down. The competing Third was wrapping around our feet.

No. We're not what you need. Follow your brethren. Join together. "We'll make it. We're almost there," I said, not knowing if I really believed that or not. *Please hurry. Push through the rock.*

I sensed the Third was growing tired. There wasn't enough of it, and it needed more energy. Slowly, it drifted back down from the ceiling, collapsing in on itself. *No, you can't give up. This is the only way to do what you were made for.* But the Third wasn't strong enough, and it was drawn to what it had experienced, knowing it could gain strength and energy by feeding off the life in the cavern. It wound its way up my leg, engulfing what was left of the Third that had stayed with me.

"Back up," I started, but it was too late.

The Third shot up my back and dug into my flesh, overpowering what had stayed there. My vision blurred, then everything darkened, and I was transported back to the beach of black sand.

But I wasn't alone. Lucas was there, waiting for me.

"It's breathtaking, isn't it?" he asked.

"Words I wouldn't have expected to hear from you," I replied, quickly looking around and trying to take stock of the situation. "You're killing it, you know. The Third and the life within the orbs."

"Oh, how little you understand, sis," he sighed. "But let me explain."

"Goody, a lecture from the crazy man," I muttered.

"A small group of explorers in the early years of humanity colonizing other areas of our solar system found something peculiar buried deep within the heart of Mars. The news about the wondrous find was buried in favor of mining Mars for its resources then pushing farther out into space, not to mention stopping the masses from panicking. At that time, we still hadn't met another alien species. But as humanity moved beyond our solar system, exploring and conquering other worlds, the small group of people who still knew about what had been found in Mars realized the find wasn't unique. Over time, the group solidified into a small conglomeration based on the shared intention of unraveling the mystery and claiming it for our own."

"But why?" I interrupted.

Lucas turned to face me. "Because we are the ones meant to unlock the secrets. In all those years spent researching and collecting information from other worlds, humanity was the only one who had been able to make contact, to finally crack the secret of the orbs."

I laughed. "Well, that's not true. You're forgetting the Darquets. Humans aren't so special after all, are they? You just made crap up to feel better about yourselves."

"Wrong. We suspected what was buried on Dar and what the Darquets had done. But they never fully used it to their full potential, either because they weren't smart enough to figure it out, or they simply didn't care. Either way, the prize was still for humanity to grab."

"Way to twist the narrative into a bunch of nonsense to suit your own twisted purposes," I muttered. "And so what's this prize? You do know you're following in the family footsteps of wormholes and taking a long time getting to the point of all of this."

Lucas stepped back and spread his arms wide. "The orbs gather and absorb an unbridled amount of power, and by unlocking the secret of communicating with the Caretakers, we can mold it into whatever we want, channel it in the right direction, and use it to take us beyond our galaxy just as they traveled to our galaxy. Humanity would be the first to explore the universe and rightfully claim our place out there in the great unknown."

"That's it? That's the great reveal? I feel like we've hashed this out before." I shook my head. "And you're wrong, you know."

His hands dropped to his sides, and tendrils of the Third moved across his skin, casting dark webs along his face. "And how is that? Do explain."

"Actually, I don't really care to, at least not until you answer another question. Why me? Why this big cult of purity worshipers? If the Third made contact with the Darquets, why not there? Or a slew of other worlds?"

Lucas paused, and for a split second, I thought I'd stumped him. But I recognized the look on his face. It was the same expression I'd seen on the Holy One when she'd been silently communicating with others.

I had a horrific realization. *Do I look that foolish when I'm communicating with Cain? Oh, merciful Saturn, I hope not.*

"Fine," Lucas said with a slight shake of his body. "An answer to your questions. For centuries upon centuries upon centuries, the Celestial Plain had tried to heal and join with the Caretakers once more, to fix what had been broken when they traveled here.

"We knew from research that the Star Eaters tried to reunite with the Caretakers. But there were disastrous results, no matter how they tried. The Caretakers had changed on a biological level, becoming so foreign to the Star Eaters that they couldn't join with them again.

"That was when the Celestial Plain appeared to a handful of worlds, trying to communicate with the indigenous life they found. But most worlds were too primitive to understand and saw them as gods or worse. When they approached humanity, we'd already uncovered what was buried on Mars and colonized a handful of worlds. So a tenuous relationship was formed."

So far, I was tracking with everything Lucas was telling me. I just wished greed hadn't gotten in the way and created generations of hateful, shortsighted individuals.

"Once the first round of scientists understood what the Star Eaters wanted, they sacrificed many in order to develop a base understanding of what would be needed to fully join with the Third—not just to be a source of food but to mentally connect and command the Third. As the experiments continued, genetic engineering was added.

"The work was so close to the answers for a long time. But the researchers had been working with genetically engineered clones that were breaking down faster with each subsequent generation. The longest-lived—of any of those early prototypes able to join with the Third—died within thirty hours. Then Dr. Ferdan Gideon had a breakthrough.

"The unnatural process of genetic engineering was the problem. While the details weren't fully understood, Dr. Gideon recognized the Third was producing a toxin when joined with the engineered clones. And not just clones but anyone who had genetic engineering in their base codes. Bioupgrades weren't an issue. So a detailed breeding program was established, along with sources of funding and the connections needed to keep everything secret.

"A Vow was made between those researchers and the Celestial Plain, a promise that once we were able to restore the Caretakers, we would be free to harness the energy of the orbs however we liked."

I stared out across the expanse of light, watching as it gently moved back and forth in an unfelt breeze. Lucas's little speech was a lot to absorb, but as I did, pairing it with what I'd learned, I came to one conclusion: the Star Eaters or, rather, the Celestial Plain had lied.

If they could lie. I had a sneaking suspicion they'd worded the Vow extremely carefully, and humans—par for the course—heard only what they wanted to. I knew the orbs were capable of absorbing and storing massive amounts of energy and that even that knowledge represented a mere fraction of what I didn't know. But they were incubators—of that I was certain. And whatever Lucas and the others thought they'd been promised, I was certain it wasn't going to come true.

Also, I was confident about one other point. If Lucas and his Third won, they would destroy what was in the orbs, just like what I'd seen happen on so many other worlds.

I took a few steps away from Lucas and raised a hand, staring at the webbing of the Third covering my own flesh. I knew I couldn't win back in the chamber. *But here... maybe.* The Third had brought me here many times, and I didn't think that was random. The Third had shown me who they truly were, and together, we were going to defeat Lucas.

30

A Job Well Done

"You know, you're forgetting one very important thing." I turned back to face him, and I couldn't wait to wipe the smug look off his face.

"What's that?" he asked.

"That they chose me and not you." I crouched down and touched the black sand, letting my fingers sink into its warmth. The Third raced down my arms and shot out across the beach, wrapping themselves around Lucas's feet. Tendrils of the Third burst through the ground around me and shot forward to capture him. I grinned in triumph as it wrapped itself around him, tightening just like the boa constrictor I'd seen at the zoo.

Triumphant, I started to stand, but resistance raced toward me through my Third, and I stumbled. The Third wrapped around Lucas, lost its luster, and hardened. I realized the Third that had joined with Lucas was fighting back, breaking through the bonds. When the Third was sliced and cut off from itself, it fell to the beach, and all I could feel was its agony at being severed.

Lucas's bonds burst, and his Third reached for me

as he extended his hands out before him. "Is that the best you can do?"

His Third reached out and pierced my flesh, wrestling me down to the ground. I screamed and writhed in agony, trying to escape, but Lucas marched forward and crouched beside me, his hands hovering above my chest. "It might have chosen you, but it should have picked me. Out of the two of us, I've always been the stronger one." He raised his hands above his head then brought them down, using the Third to push me into the ground.

Sand poured in around my face and into my mouth, grating against my eyes. I tried to struggle, to use the Third to fight back, but then I realized I was guilty of using the Third just like Lucas, just like the Darquets. Forcing myself to relax, I tried to still my thoughts and push back against the panic. *No. I won't die like this. I won't let my fears defeat me.* Instead, I focused on how warm and comforting the sand could feel, and I reached out to what was left of my Third, asking it to join with Lucas's.

This wasn't what you were created for. You are the Caretaker, the one who nurtures and gives to the light within the Path Makers. Those of the Celestial Plain did not abandon you. They're waiting for you. They've been trying to reach out, to reconnect, but couldn't do it on their own. But you have me. Use me to be the bridge. Let me help you fulfill your purpose. Let me help reconnect you to the Celestial Plain. If you don't, what you're doing will only ensure the destruction of the Path Makers, the last of those that came with you.

I waited for a response, any kind of sense that the Third understood what I was offering. It didn't come.

Please. Use me. The Celestial Light is waiting for you. But we need to work together.

The silence was deafening, and I realized I'd failed. Lucas had been right all along. He'd been strong, and I'd been weak. Pops had realized that. He'd hidden my memories and turned his attentions to Lucas because he knew I wouldn't be able to do what was necessary. I only wished they'd truly understood what they had been working toward, not some twisted perception of greed and vanity. Sorrow and guilt and despair overwhelmed me, and I decided the time had come to accept reality and succumb to my fate.

The pressure of the sand closing in around me pushed me farther down, and I couldn't help but wonder if dying there would trap me in that place. *Is it another plane of existence? Shared hallucinations because of the joining with the Third? Will Cain even begin to understand what I tried to do, the sacrifice I'm willing to make?*

My thoughts spiraled into a chaotic mess until I felt something pushing through the sand. It brushed up against me then wrapped around my hands and pulled. I sat up, coughing and sputtering, trying to clear my eyes and mouth.

"Union. Healing. Light."

I heard those words loud and clear and couldn't help but grin like a fool. Wiping away the last of the sand, I saw myself sitting across from me, exactly what I'd experienced on Dar. Twinkling blue lights darted through the air around us. I reached out, letting the lights settle on my hand as I realized Lucas was rushing toward us, his face a twisted nightmare of fury.

"No! I won't let you!" he shouted.

I started to stand, ready to do what I could to defend my reflection, but it lifted its hand, and a gigantic wall of the Third shot up out of the ground and fell toward Lucas before he could get out of its way. It wrapped itself around him like a large net, tightening and tightening until Lucas couldn't move.

"What will you do with him?" I asked.

"Emptiness. Ending. Beginning."

"Not really clearing it up for me. But you know you can't trust him, right?"

My reflection didn't answer but instead reached out and touched my forehead. An overwhelming sense of peace flooded my body, and I knew the Third understood.

"Union. Healing. Light."

I let my eyes drift shut and just sat there, soaking in the sense of peace, the sense of unity and purpose. When I eventually opened my eyes again, I was back in the cavern.

Once again receding from the bodies strewn about, the Third was coming together to reform the thick, treelike trunk. Tendrils wrapped around themselves, and it grew taller and taller until it touched the ceiling. With its united purpose, it had no need to find the cracks and crevices but simply pushed, and bits and pieces of the rock fell to the ground.

I brushed one hand over the last of the Third wrapped around my other hand. *Go, and thank you.* After a rush of warmth, a few blue lights emerged and fluttered around my head. It slid off my hand and moved across the floor to join with the others. The sight was marvelous and terrifying all wrapped up together as I watched the Third punch through the rock.

"Mahia, we need to move," Cain said softly. He grabbed my arms and pulled me back as a large piece of the ceiling crashed down where we'd been standing. He guided me over to the edge of the cavern where Ochoa was helping Miles. "We need to get out of here."

"The way we came is blocked by the Sun Worshipers. Don't know how many are left," Miles said and coughed, little drops of blood splattering against the face shield of his suit. "But I think—"

"Gather up everyone you can," I said, interrupting Miles. "I can send them through into the cavern while we wait this out." I didn't know how many I could take, and a quick look around confirmed my sinking suspicions. Not many were left alive, able to make it. Another chunk of the roof collapsed, and I turned and buried my head in Cain's chest, not wanting to see the destruction being wreaked on those lying prone around the cavern.

"Stay here," he whispered. "Stay with Miles. Ochoa and I will get who we can."

I nodded, pulled back, and turned my attention to Miles. "Are you okay?"

He nodded and gave me a thumbs-up. "The suit's already hard at work. I'll be good to go in a few. But we need a faster way to get—"

"I'll work as fast as I can. I promise."

I heard a shout then the pop of weapons firing. I spun around, searching widely for Cain. He'd worked his way toward the entrance and was crouched down in a defensive posture. Ochoa was in front of him, wrestling another woman for control over a gun. In the struggle, the gun went off again, and the woman took advantage of the opening and wrapped an arm around Ochoa's neck.

"Orion, you need to stop this. Right now. Or else she's dead. Then Mr. Suren ed-Turen. Then the thorn in my side."

I pulled away from Miles and walked into the light, keeping an eye on the cracks in the ceiling. The Third was almost through to the surface, so all I needed to do was stall. "I don't think so, Commandant."

"You don't know what you're doing," she snapped. "The years I've sacrificed and done what was necessary in order to stop the Star Eaters, and now you're just picking up where Lucas and the others left off."

"That's where you're wrong. I wasn't helping Lucas—never was. But I am keeping a promise I made." I took a few more steps closer, one eye on the ceiling and another on Yilmaz. "Besides, if that was what you truly thought of me, why didn't you kill me when you had the chance?" I held up a hand. "Rhetorical question. I'll answer it for you. It was because *you* were helping Lucas. Oh, you might not have known it, but you and Dr. Ashter were just as blinded by your greed as everyone else. And so you let me live in order to watch and see what I would do, where I would go."

"You stupid woman. You've stumbled into something you can't even begin to fathom," Yilmaz hissed.

The Third pulled back and, with one last push, broke through to the surface. Dirt and globs of slime rained down around us, and I really hoped that, after everything Cain and I had been through, we wouldn't be taken out by some radioactive slime ball. Ochoa took advantage of the disruption and snapped her head back, landing a solid blow against Yilmaz while Cain simultaneously jumped forward and tackled them. The three of them fell to the ground, and together, Cain and Ochoa were able to subdue Yilmaz.

Sunlight poured through the hole in the ceiling, and I sensed the Third hesitating. Knowing Ochoa and Cain had Yilmaz in hand, I turned my attention back to the pillar. *Use me. Let me be the bridge. This is what you've been hoping for.* A part of the Third spun off of itself and reached out to me, gently sliding over my shoulders and down my back then across my arms and hands.

"If you do this, you're going to destroy us all!" Yilmaz shouted. "You've got to stop—"

Using the butt of one of the weapons, Cain hit her hard. Yilmaz toppled forward and was silent.

I tilted my head back and stared up through the hole at the light trying to filter down into the cavern. "The Ray of Ascension is waiting for you." I had a sneaking suspicion we'd punctured a hole exactly where the Two had said they would be waiting.

After a flash of white light, when I could see again, the Two were standing beside me. "The Ray of Ascension must be completed."

The pillar of the Third shivered, and I sensed anticipation, fear, and a fair amount of longing. Part of it separated from the whole and formed a Ray of Requirement, complete with twinkling blue lights dancing along the glyph.

The Two turned to me and bowed. "The Vows are now complete. The offspring of Wats Hawking Orion has gifted the Caretakers with union. The Ray of Ascension can now be fulfilled."

I moved to Cain and the others. "I'd say we need to get out of here. Pronto."

"I think it's safe to assume the tunnels are clear. Whoever was in there was…" She struggled for the word.

I helped her out. "Eaten. It's a fair description."

"Fine. Eaten, then. We can use the tunnels and get back to the surface."

Yilmaz groaned and rolled over. "Fools. Because of you and your stupid family, the known worlds are going to be destroyed."

I looked down at her and shrugged. "Don't think so, but whatever. You keep holding onto your delusions."

Yilmaz struggled to get up, and Ochoa reached out and yanked her to her feet but quickly snapped on a pair of restraints. "If Lucas hadn't stolen what belonged to the IGJ, then we'd still have something we could use to fight what's coming. But now, we don't. And you've killed him, and we can't get the intel on what he did with the weapon."

I turned to gape at the woman. "Wait. No… are you telling me that—"

A tremor ran through the floor, and I noticed the orbs had continued to crack open. The Two were transferring their light to the Third, thus finishing the Ray of Ascension.

"The gates are open, and all shall burn with its glory," Yilmaz murmured. "Let the light shine radiant. Let the stars burn bright as the gates are opened."

Miles had limped over to us by that point, and he tapped me on the shoulder. "I really think we need to get out of here."

"Agreed, but I don't think—"

"If you'd let me finish before, I was going to tell you. The scramblers they set up are out."

"So if we get to the surface, they can send down shuttles?" I asked.

Miles grinned. "Even better. You up for a good old-fashioned round of zap 'n' roll?"

31

And the Other Shoe Drops

Miles and his miraculous fleet of ships.

The *SnapDragon* was the next generation of ship based on the *Samaritan* and its sister ships. The design was similar enough that maneuvering through the decks was fairly easy. We'd left Epo-5 in the nick of time. The energy generated by the hatching of the baby Star Eaters—that nickname was really hard to let go of—was causing massive earthquakes across the entire planet. I didn't understand a lot, but I hoped the Third and the Two were all at peace. My suspicion was that the Third had died during the final transference of energy, for I couldn't sense its presence. Nor could I make my hand glow. But I wasn't going to be surprised if some permanent biological changes had taken place.

Miles and the rest of those who'd survived Epo-5 were going to be holed up in sick bay for at least a week. And the IGJ on Yilmaz's side had around-the-clock guards, along with Ochoa firmly keeping an eye out for any shenanigans.

Cain—*blow me over*—checked in with Miles every

day. Through all the craziness, they'd somehow finally reached an understanding. While I knew some issues between them would simply scar over and never fully heal, I was relieved to see them mending bridges. I'd gone with Cain on one of those visits, and their conversation had drifted off into years gone by and Elea. I'd quietly left them to reminisce.

Lio was inbound, and I'd updated him from my end. I was anxious to see him in person and figure out what to do with our unexpected guest.

Yilmaz had been treated and locked up in one of the nicer hab-units. I'd wanted her in the brig, nice and secure, but Miles had argued against that. Ultimately, he was right. On Epo-5, she hadn't done anything wrong, and we needed to come to some type of agreement. I know what Cain wanted to do. I could hear the dark thoughts roaming around in his head. But so far, he'd kept quiet on the issue.

I found myself standing outside her hab-unit occasionally and had finally worked up the nerve to see her. I was sure she wasn't a happy camper and had already plotted ten different ways of getting revenge. Ochoa had encouraged me to see Yilmaz, to listen and gather intel but to stay quiet when asked any questions. And she'd assured me Yilmaz would be a fool to try anything right then. She was outnumbered and knew it. If she attacked me, no way was she going to get off the ship alive.

"Open it up," I said with a sigh.

The guards complied, and the door whooshed open. I stepped in, half expecting Yilmaz to try to attack me, but she was sitting at the table, sipping from a mug.

"Ms. Orion, please come in and have a seat," she said. "Do you want something to drink?"

I picked my jaw up off the floor and shook my head. "No, thanks. And I'll stand, thank you." I know Ochoa said not to answer questions, but I wanted to play at least a little polite if Yilmaz was going to.

She shrugged. "To each their own."

When she didn't say anything else, I said, "I thought you'd want to see me."

"Yes. Are you aware of what you've done?" she asked.

I rolled my eyes. "Not again. Haven't been paying attention, have you?"

She leaned back in her chair. "Of course. And I'm seeing where I've made a few... errors in judgment." She wrapped her hands around the mug and stared at the steam wafting up off the liquid. "I believe that you believe you've just done something... worthy. Something good. Yes?"

I crossed my arms over my chest and stared at her.

"Fine." She took another drink then stood. "Your father was a brilliant man—shortsighted by his upbringing, though. But I can't lay all the blame at his feet. I certainly could've done more—reached out to him sooner or even you, for that matter. Perhaps all of this could've been avoided. But here we are, and now we must do what needs doing in order to salvage the situation."

"What are you talking about?"

"The Star Eaters. What you've unleashed."

I narrowed my eyes. "I haven't *unleashed* anything. I've helped restore the Third to what they were meant to be. And perhaps if more people had actually tried to understand what was going on instead of only seeing their situation as something they could profit from, more of the Third or the baby Star Eaters could've been saved."

"Thank the gods they weren't." Yilmaz snorted. "What do you know about the Star Eaters? Really? Beyond what they've obviously wanted you to know?"

And I'm done. "Nope," I said and turned to leave. "The games are over. Everything is finished. You've lost, and I've won. Deal with it."

"Where do you think Lucas got the tech he needed to start a war?" Yilmaz asked.

I stopped. *What was it she'd said?* "You said he stole it"—I turned around—"from *you*." In the rush to leave Epo-5 and look after all the wounded, I'd forgotten that little detail. *Well, not really so little, was it?* "How could you even develop something like that? Why? Tell me why? Was it because you feared the Jumjul?"

Yilmaz shook her head. "Good gods, no. We built it to protect ourselves from the Star Eaters in the event something like what you helped facilitate should happen. We built the weapon in order to destroy the Star Eaters before they could complete their Ascension."

"Why? For Pluto's sake, why?"

Yilmaz turned away from me and walked over to the small viewing window. She stared out into the darkness of space. "Because the Star Eaters have been trying to get home. For a millennium, they've been trying. And now that there are enough of them, they're going to do just that. But in doing so, they're going to destroy our galaxy. Because that's what they do. Haven't you ever wondered how they ended up with the moniker of Star Eaters?"

A couch was only a few steps away, and I moved to it and plopped down. "No."

"They consume light, energy. And what's the biggest, brightest source they can find?"

"No."

"And you've just given them the strength to do what they need. To gather enough energy to go home."

"No." I was a broken record at that point.

"The Gatekeepers of Opali-Poli have known this truth from the beginning, and all who take on the mantle have worked to prevent exactly what you've just done."

I looked at her in disbelief. "And you don't think telling me all of this when we had our little chats on the *Justus* would've been helpful?"

"I believed you were working with your brother. That you were just another Sun Worshiper in disguise."

"But I don't sport their little tattoo. And I surely wasn't involved with them. You can't tell me the IGJ couldn't have parsed that from the shiploads of info you keep on everyone," I countered.

She shrugged. "Like I said, your father was brilliant. The tattoo was a dead giveaway. I was working under the assumption he'd set you up as a type of… sleeper. Throw us off the track with Lucas and bide his time until you were activated."

"I don't believe you," I said as I got up and started pacing. "Nothing you told me on the *Justus* makes me believe you now. You're working some other angle."

<What's wrong? Where are you? If that woman has done anything—>

<Physically, I'm fine. I'll be through in just a bit.>

<I'm coming to you.>

I knew I couldn't argue with him. I could sense his rage and protectiveness clearly through our connection.

"And why do you think I'd just bring you in on the truth of the matter if I thought you were working with your brother?"

"Then what about Triton? And the mad scientist routine you did with me?" I asked.

"If we could understand what it was the Star Eaters wanted, then we could figure out how to stop them."

I snorted. "Don't take me for being stupid now, of all times. Pops killed all those people on the *Rapscallion* with that bacteria Mrs. Gol almost killed me with. So wrong answer. What were you doing with Triton?"

Yilmaz shook her head. "I don't know why your father killed them, not when he was still working toward the same goal. But the bacteria… That was just a temporary stopgap. The Star Eaters would've found another group of people to work with in time. No, we were looking for a permanent answer, a way to kill the Star Eaters themselves."

"And the weapon Lucas stole?"

"A last resort. Do you really think I wanted to blow up an entire planet? If there was a way to destroy the Star Eaters without the casualties, I had to try. But in the end, I would've done whatever was needed."

"Sacrificing the many for the good of the one," I

murmured, remembering the obscure religious motto Yilmaz subscribed to.

"Exactly," Yilmaz said.

"But the Third was doing what it was created to do, to care for and nurture the orbs. The Path Mak—"

Yilmaz stared at me.

"They aren't little baby Star Eaters, are they?"

She shook her head. "No."

"Then what?"

"For that, you're going to have to have a chat with the Eeri."

I snorted. "Yeah, right. Like that's going to happen."

"If you give me access, I can set up the meeting. Whenever you want. A select group of individuals have been in negotiations with the Eeri, and I've used those channels to discuss their views on the Star Eaters. It appears we have a lot in common."

"Forget it," I said and stormed out of the room. As the door closed, I felt a serious cloud of doubt descend.

Cain rounded the corner, and I hurried over to him.

"She's playing games with you," he said. "Don't let her get in your head."

Too late for that.

32

We're Off to See the... Eeri

By the time the *Samaritan* arrived, I was convinced that Yilmaz was playing another game, that she was too stubborn to concede defeat. But when Lio came over to the *SnapDragon*, accompanied by the Master Glipglow, I realized the commandant might've been telling the truth.

We didn't waste any time and gathered in the medical suite Miles had overtaken. I was fairly sure he was well enough to leave but was relishing all the attention from his crew. If you listened to the gossip, he sounded like the hero of the story. But I wasn't trying to begrudge him any glory. If not for Miles, Lucas would've gotten his way. But it was Miles. Of course the story was going to be "embellished."

"I sent word as soon as I received your updates, to everyone I knew. The Jumjul are cautiously optimistic, and I'm told they're sitting down to talk. But they're also demanding proof too. I'm not sure how we're going to accomplish that. Any suggestions?" Lio asked.

Ochoa and Miles batted around a few ideas, but I kept silent. Politics wasn't my world. Nor did I want it to be.

"We must speak with you," the master whispered, leaning over. *Whispered* might not have been the most accurate word, but he tried to be discreet.

"I really have to apologize," I said. "I didn't mean to drag you into all of this. I was looking for some answers, but I've already got them. Between the *Samaritan* and the *SnapDragon*, I'm sure we can make arrangements to get you wherever you need to go."

His lower jaws opened and snapped shut, and he looked extremely affronted.

<I'd hear him out. Give him that dignity,> Cain offered.

I glanced over at Miles and the others, still discussing the Jumjul and how they were going to prove they'd defeated Lucas.

"My apologies, Master. That was rude and short-sighted of me. Please…" I stood and gestured for him to follow me.

Cain stood as well, and when I tried to protest, he shook his head. *<This is my mother's talent, not mine.>*

We moved to the other side of the room, and the master reached out to activate one of the screens. His nail tips rested on the interface pad, and a plethora of data appeared.

"We analyzed the data you sent and found several alarming similarities in a database that's long lain dormant."

"That would make sense, considering there were—"

Cain nudged me in the side, and I snapped my mouth shut.

<I'm just on edge because of Yilmaz,> I said.

<And I told you not to let her get in your head.>

That was easier said than done, but the master hadn't noticed my interruption and had continued talking.

"We consulted with another master and reached the same conclusion. There are minute but distinct changes in several of your base pairs across a wide range of chromosomes. These aren't splices or modifications like what is common practice through genetic engineering or bioupgrade technology."

He had my attention.

The master brought up a new screen with images and medical jargon I didn't understand, beyond the fact that what he was trying to tell me wasn't a good thing.

"These changes were layered on top of your DNA, and they're cannibalizing what they're taking from you and crafting something entirely different. You can see here on this chromosome and these other two, the subtle changes taking place. We need to redraw the samples and compare what changes have occurred. We would like to establish a base rate of the changes taking place and monitor you for any adverse reactions or larger biological changes that may be happening."

"You will," Miles spoke up from behind us. He'd gotten out of his bed and joined us. "Whatever you need, just make a list, and I'll see to it that you get it."

"You mentioned a database," Cain said.

The Glipglow nodded. "Yes, an old one. We wouldn't have considered it except for the unusual nature of what we were witnessing."

"So you're saying you've seen this before? On your world? The Glipglows tried to help the Star Eaters too?" I asked.

The master's tail curled around his feet. "No, not the Glipglows but an old trading partner."

I closed my eyes, knowing what he was going to say before he did.

"The Eeri."

"No. Absolutely not!" Cain exploded. "I don't know how, but Yilmaz is only—"

<Enough,> I said.

Cain glared at me.

"Care to fill me in?" Miles asked.

"I was going to, I swear. I was just waiting for the rest of you to finish hashing out your end of things," I whispered. I looked at the master. "Thank you. I really appreciate your help. I'll do whatever you need. I want to understand what's changed or…" *Is still changing.* But I didn't want to say that out loud.

"Miles? Will you get the others?"

He nodded and ushered the others over to the screen. I had the master fill them in and expand a little on the topic. While I might not have understood it all, the others might. Or at least it might spark something else they didn't realize they knew.

"I would assume this ties in with what you were able to do down in the tunnels," Ochoa said when the master finished. "How you were able to use the glyphs and communicate with the Third."

I nodded. "I would, too, but the more important connection is the Eeri." Saying their name felt wrong after such a long time of hating them. "Pops went to the Eeri for some reason. He talked about it in his journals." I wished those hadn't been lost in all the chaos. "And I know now it wasn't for the reason we all thought. It was all wrapped up with the Star Eaters. And now, Yilmaz has brought them up, alluding to some terrible disaster that I've allowed the Star Eaters to do. Then this. The Eeri know what we don't." I quickly filled everyone in on what Yilmaz had told me.

"You're laying trust at the feet of a woman I wouldn't," Cain snapped. His tail whipped back and forth.

"While I share Cain's sentiment about the commandant," Ochoa said, "I also believe Yilmaz wouldn't have brought it up if there wasn't a nugget of truth in there. I'm not saying she's trustworthy, but if there's a chance she could be right, then we need to investigate it."

My chest tightened, and I turned and walked over to the large viewing field in the room.

Cain joined me and wrapped his arms around me. "What's wrong?"

"If Yilmaz is right or even partially right, then... I was a fool. I let the Star Eaters and the Third manipulate me into doing something terrible."

"You can't think like that," Cain murmured. "You were helping them. You were acting out of compassion and kindness. And if there is more going on than we know, we'll figure it out and deal with it."

"Amen to that," Miles said. "Look, I can guess what's brewing inside that pretty little head of yours. You're blaming yourself. Going to start thinking a whole bunch of what-if scenarios. Well, don't. You didn't do anything wrong. You helped stop Lucas and a war with the Jumjul. And if the Star Eaters pose a serious threat, then now we know. And what we know, we can take care of."

I gave him a weak smile. "Thanks."

"Is that it?" Cain asked, to which Miles nodded. "Then go away," Cain said but without any malice in his words, just lighthearted teasing.

"I really thought this was all over," I said.

"I know, but you're not alone," he replied.

<I guess we're going to go meet the Eeri. Can't say I'm too thrilled about it all.>

<Just another day in the life of Mahia Orion,> Cain teased.

I looked out into the darkness of space and tried to smile. *Another day in my crazy life. None of what you did gave me that normal life, did it, Pops?* But as I began to consider what our next steps should be, I realized one thing: I really wasn't all that sad. I was getting used to these crazy adventures.

Thank you for reading *The Secrets of Epo-5*!

Don't miss out on what happens next for Mahia and Cain or explore what other titles I have to offer. You can sign-up to stay in touch through my newsletter at:

elizabethknollston.com

You can also follow me on social media at:
facebook.com/elizabethknollston
twitter.com/EKnollston

Look for the epic conclusion of the
The Three-Fold Suns Series

The Celestial Light

and discover the twists and turns that are on the horizon!

Acknowledgements

Looking at the world and the universe beyond with questioning eyes and a curious mind was because of the encouragement I received from my parents. Without their love and support, this journey of becoming an author wouldn't have been possible. I will forever cherish the memories of adventurous vacations, the love of reading, and the support of being who I am.

I've been fortunate to find so many others along this journey to share my love of imagination and far-flung worlds. Being able to surround myself with people who have cheered me on to write and share the stories I create has been a wonderful gift of friendship and found family.

All I can say is an endless string of deep and grateful thank yous to everyone who has helped and supported me along the way.

And without the wonderful editors at Red Adept Editing, this story wouldn't be where it is today without all of their hard work to push me and help polish this story! Thank you so much for all that you have done.

Thank you to all of my readers for your interest in my work and believing in me! I am so grateful for your taking a chance on this book and leaving your kind words of reviews and encouragement. And I look forward to writing more far-flung adventures to share with you all!

About the Author

Elizabeth Knollston collects dragons. No, they're not real. But if you know of a mad scientist or genetic engineer who's working on the real deal, be sure to let her know. She would dearly love to collect star ships too, but those won't fit in her garage.

Her (overactive) imagination is credit to her parents, who outrageously encouraged her poor spending habits of buying too many books. And just a side note—if you ever plan on moving, book collecting isn't helpful.

In another life, Elizabeth dreamed of becoming an archaeologist, but a fascinating and rewarding job as a therapeutic horseback riding instructor derailed those plans. When Elizabeth isn't wondering about being on a manned mission to Mars, she enjoys bugging her dog, battling the weeds in her garden, and being a productive member of society.